SHIRLEY HAILSTOCK

HARLEQUIN® KIMANI™ ROMANCE

To my dear and supportive friend and
fellow author Candice Poarch.

Recycling programs
for this product may
not exist in your area.

ISBN-13: 978-0-373-86371-6

SOMEONE LIKE YOU

H HARLEQUIN®

Printed in U.S.A. ™ www.Harlequin.com

Dear Reader,

Theresa (Teddy) Granville is Diana's friend and partner from *His Love Match,* the first book in the Weddings by Diana series. It wasn't long into writing about this character that I knew Teddy had to have her own story and her own wonderful hero in Adam Sullivan. From my own experience working in a bridal shop, I knew how important the mother of the bride *and* the mother of the groom are to the nuptials of their children.

It doesn't matter how educated or intelligent the parents are. When it comes to their children, logic is what they say it is. And, thus, the meddling mothers show their tail feathers.

It's great fun to watch as the women *think* they're pulling their children's strings. But, as it turns out, Teddy and Adam have other plans....

Happy endings,

Shirley Hailstock

Chapter 1

Blind date! Theresa Granville, Teddy to her friends, drummed her long red fingernails on the white tablecloth. She was waiting for Adam Sullivan, a man she'd never met, and she could just as easily spend the rest of her life happily oblivious of his existence. But that was not to be. She'd been set up. Teddy hated blind dates and she didn't need anyone to find her a man, especially not her *mother*. The truth was, she was capable of meeting men on her own and dated often. But she'd been goaded into agreeing to have dinner with Adam Sullivan. Since she didn't like to go back on her word, she was stuck.

The restaurant was crowded for a Thursday night in Princeton. It was fall and the majority of the university students returned a month ago. Most of the restaurant's patrons were around the bar cheering on some sports team's efforts to statistically capture a spot in the history books. Teddy had long since stopped hearing the triumphs and groans of their participation in the televised game. She'd relegated the sound to white noise. Her attention was on the restaurant's entrance. From her solitary perch on the second-floor dining area, where private parties were usually held, maybe she'd be able to spot her date when *and if* he arrived. Maybe he hated blind dates, too. And Teddy would feel no disappointment at being stood up. If she didn't have to gently explain to her mother yet again why she didn't want to be set up, she wouldn't be here, either.

Frowning, she watched a short guy with round-rimmed glasses enter. Her fingers went to the phone in her pocket. Diana, her friend and business partner, was only a call away. The two had worked out a signal if Teddy wanted or *needed* to be rescued.

Again, she glanced at the man below, taking in his height or lack of it. One of Teddy's requirements in a man was height. At five feet nine inches, she didn't want to stand with a man whose head only reached her breasts. Thankfully, Mr. Glasses lifted his hand, acknowledging his party, and joined a group at the end of the bar. She breathed a sigh of relief that he wasn't her blind date.

Three other singles and two couples came in before the seven o'clock appointed hour. Then *he* walked in right as the clock struck the hour. Teddy did a double take when she saw him. Shaking her head, she immediately rejected him as someone who'd never need a blind date. He couldn't be the one. Her mother didn't have taste that good. Except for her father, who was still a handsome man in his fifties, the men her mother usually chose looked like the round-rimmed-glasses guy.

For a moment Teddy wished her date *was* the man at the door. Leaning over the banister, she watched the stranger move toward the receptionist. The two had a short conversation and she checked her seating chart. Then she shook her head. As she gathered a couple of menus and led him toward a table, the room was momentarily quiet, allowing Teddy to overhear her own name.

"I'll bring Ms. Granville over as soon as she arrives, sir," the woman said.

Teddy gasped. Her stomach lurched and her heart jumped into her throat. This couldn't be Adam Sullivan. He was gorgeous. Where did her mother find *him?* He was tall, at least six foot two. His shoulders were broad enough to rest any available head and for a moment she thought of hers resting there. Why would this guy need to be set up on a date? It took her a moment to gather herself. This was still a blind date and, as far as she knew, the two of them had nothing in common. Meeting him could be a disaster despite his looks. In fact, she expected it was. A man this good-looking could stand on his own. Yes, she decided, there had to be something wrong with him.

Rising, Teddy tucked her handbag under her arm and left her solitary seat in the upper balcony. She took the back stairs that led to the main floor. Entering through the bar, she was assaulted by the noise. The crowd was wall-to-wall and a whoop of pleasure went up as she wove her way toward the crowd. She smiled here and there, gently warding off interested men. At the entrance to the restaurant section, she peered through the vertical columns separating the dining area from the den of sports enthusiasts.

Adam Sullivan had no smile. He looked comfortably about, taking in the other diners as if he'd need to recall their exact positions at some later date. He wore an open-neck shirt and dark jacket. Masculinity exuded from him. Even sitting alone, he appeared in command. He was clean-shaven with dark tanned skin, hair cut close and neat, no mustache. Other than the I'm-in-command aura he wore, there was something else about him. Something that said "Sex!"

That's what it was. Sex appeal. Tons of it. More than any one person should be allotted. From across the room, he had her breathing hard and all she'd done was look at him. She wondered again what was wrong with him that he'd even consider meeting a stranger for dinner. He didn't look as if he needed help in finding companionship. From the stares of the other women in the room, they'd gladly leave their own parties to join his.

The receptionist was away. Teddy passed the receptionist's station and walked with measured steps toward his table. He looked up as she approached. His face remained serious, no smile, no outward sign of approval. She was slightly disappointed and a little bit insulted.

"Theresa Granville?" he asked as he stood.

She nodded, looking him straight in the eye. He

passed the height test. Teddy wore five-inch spiked heels and if she took them off, she'd only reach his chin.

"Adam Sullivan," he identified himself.

Teddy extended her hand. He took it in his larger one. It was warm and strong. She'd never been one to use clichés to describe people, but there was no other way to think of him.

Adam Sullivan was *sexy as hell.*

Conversations clashed with plates and silverware, bringing the sound in the room to a wealth of indistinct noise. Occasionally there was a burst of laughter from the bar area that drew everyone's attention for a few seconds.

Adam pulled out a chair next to his and Teddy took a seat. She waited for him to say something, but the moment stretched into awkwardness. She thumbed the edge of the menu but did not pick it up.

"Why did you agree to this?" she finally asked.

"To what?" His eyebrows rose as if he hadn't understood her question.

"Going on a blind date."

"Are you blind?"

She rolled her eyes. So that was his problem. His humor sucked. What else was wrong with him?

Then she saw a slight smile lift the corners of his mouth. Not a full smile, but it made her wonder what one would look like.

"Sorry, I had to say that. I hoped it would break the ice."

"So blind dates aren't your thing, either?" Teddy said.

"I'd rather be boiled in oil."

"Well," Teddy said, "I guess that sums it up." She felt slightly put out, even though she felt the same. She'd never been turned down for a date and frankly she didn't really like this guy. And even though she didn't want a blind date, she wanted to be the one to make the decision to end the night. "I suppose we should just shake hands and return to our lives."

She waited again for him to do something, but he seemed to be waiting for her. She stood up and extended her hand. He stood and took it.

"It was nice meeting you," he said.

His voice was perfunctory. There was nothing nice about the meeting, but Teddy was relieved she wasn't going to have to sit through an awkward getting-to-know-you discussion.

"Sorry it didn't work out." She wasn't really sorry, but the words seemed appropriate. And she wouldn't have to call Diana for rescue. As she picked up her purse, her stomach growled.

"It wouldn't have worked anyway," he said. "You're not my usual type."

"What type is that?" For some reason Teddy's back went up. She'd never been dismissed before she even got a chance to prove herself.

"You're too tall, too intelligent."

Teddy blinked. Was he real? "You can tell my intelligence level from a couple of sentences?"

"My mother gave me a little information," he explained.

Teddy's mother had told her nothing. "I see. You're

looking for arm candy. Petite, long wavy hair maybe, big brown eyes. The kind you could get lost in." She paused, giving him a moment.

"Someone who isn't very smart, but good in bed," he admitted.

Not to be waylaid by the good-in-bed comment, Teddy asked, "So I'm being dumped because of my height?"

"Not exactly dumped," he said.

Teddy took a breath and calmed down. She smiled sarcastically. "You're right. I am not the one. I'm not arm candy and I don't want a man who is. No matter how good-looking you are, I prefer a man I can talk to both before *and* after sex." She hooked her purse farther up on her shoulder. "And I am not just good in bed, I'm *great* in bed."

Pivoting on her high heels, she moved away from the table. She'd only taken a step when he called her name. "Theresa?"

She turned back.

"I probably shouldn't have said that. It's been a long day and I've forgotten my manners."

"Is that an apology?"

He nodded.

She had the feeling that he rarely apologized. He was a man in command. She could tell he was confident and obviously chose his own road. This date orchestrated by his mother and her mother was outside his developed character.

"Teddy," she said. "Everyone calls me Teddy."

"Teddy," he repeated. "Since you're obviously hungry, and we're already here—" he spread his hands encompassing the room "—we might as well eat. That way I can answer truthfully when asked how my night went."

"It hasn't begun on a high note. You sure you don't want to stop here? If we go on, things could get worse."

He laughed. The sound was deep and infectious, but Teddy refused to join in. She kept her features straight and unsmiling.

Teddy shrugged and returned to her seat. Undoubtedly, she'd be questioned, too. They ordered, and as she cut into a prime rib so tender she could have used a butter knife, Adam opened the conversation.

"While I was arguing with my…" He stopped. "I hear you're in the wedding business."

Teddy didn't like his tone. She nodded. "I design wedding gowns and I'm a partner in a wedding consulting firm."

"So you believe in orange blossoms and till death do us part?"

She refused to rise to the obvious bait. "Orange blossoms would be very expensive on this coast. But there are some brides who insist on them."

He raised a single eyebrow and sipped his drink.

"I take it you are a nonbeliever?" Teddy asked.

"I'm a realist. I've seen too many of my friends walk down that aisle only to end up hating the person they vowed to love."

Teddy was in trouble. She should have taken the opportunity to walk out the door when she had it. Now she was as stuck here for as long as the meal lasted.

"You've been married," she stated. He had all the earmarks of a man who'd been hurt in a relationship, but his tone regarding orange blossoms told her he'd been down that aisle himself. His nod was barely perceptible.

"And you hate her now?"

He shook his head. "Quite the opposite. We're very good friends."

She frowned. This was an exception to the rule of divorce. "What happened?" she asked, realizing it was probably the wrong question, but it was already out.

He spread his hands and hunched his shoulders. "We were too young. We got married for all the wrong reasons. Mainly, we didn't know each other, didn't understand that our dreams weren't the same."

"What was her dream?"

He smiled. Teddy liked it. It was the good-memory smile, the one that appears when a person looks back and only he understands the happy place he's entered. She was glad he had good memories of his marriage. She'd seen her share of people who only remembered the wedge that separated their relationship and not what created it.

"Her dream was to be an actress." He took a moment to eat some of his steak before continuing. "After our divorce, she moved to L.A. and got a part on a soap opera."

A light dawned in Teddy's brain. *Chelsea Sullivan?* She rolled the name around in her mind. "You were married to Chelsea Sullivan?"

He nodded. "She kept the name."

Chelsea Sullivan was the lead actress on the top daytime television program. From what Teddy read in the entertainment magazines, she was about to move her career to feature films.

He sat back in his chair. "And you? What did you dream of being?"

"I have my dream. I wanted my own design business."

He smiled fully. "Then you're ahead of most of the world. You have everything."

Not everything, she thought. Her partner, Diana, married last year, and while the two of them had been friends for years, Teddy wondered at the happy changes she saw in her friend. There was a newness, a happiness that hadn't been there before. While they both loved the work, for Diana there was something more to look forward to at the end of the day. Teddy had begun to wonder what she was missing.

But as she sat across from Adam, Teddy wondered how anyone could talk him into meeting someone whose business was weddings when he didn't believe in them. And so far she was sure he wasn't the one for her.

"What about marriage?" he asked.

The word hit her like a spray of ice water. "Me? Married? Never made the trip."

"I see," he said. "You give the story to everyone else but stand clear of it yourself?"

"You say that as if it was by design."

"Is it?" Adam asked. He stared straight at her.

"No, I suppose I'm the cliché," Teddy said.

"Always a bridesmaid, never a bride?"

She shook her head. "I haven't met the right man, yet."

"But your parents are determined to find him for you if you don't do it yourself?"

Teddy nodded. "My mother for sure. But isn't marriage a taboo conversation for people on a first date?" Teddy asked.

"I suppose it is, but we decided this is dinner, not a date." He laughed again. This time Teddy laughed, too.

"What do you do?" she asked. In speaking with her mother, she'd never asked anything about him. She'd been too busy arguing that she didn't want to go on a blind date to think about his profession.

"Investments. I own a brokerage house."

She was impressed, but kept it off her face and out of her voice. "So, I deal in dreams and you in cold, hard cash."

"Not cold or hard. Just ones and zeros." There was no censure in his voice. It was also devoid of pride or arrogance.

"Computer transactions." Teddy nodded, understanding that everything today was done on a small machine you could put in your pocket.

"Actual money is on the way out." He turned to her, pulling his chair an inch closer. "How much money do you have in your purse right now?"

Teddy glanced in surprise at the clutch bag that lay on the table. Tossing her head, she said, "Enough for a taxi and a phone call."

Adam smiled. It was the first time since they met that his face showed any emotion. "I remember hearing my mother telling me about taxi fare and carrying cash when she and my father were dating. Of course, their generation can remember life before cell phones."

"I got that story from my father. He wanted to make sure I could get home or at least call if some guy got out of hand. He said I could lose the phone or forget to charge the battery."

"Did it ever happen?" he asked.

"The phone, no. The date, nothing I couldn't handle."

Adam gave her a long stare. She wondered what he was thinking. She hadn't issued a challenge, yet she felt as if he was thinking of one.

"What about you? Any sisters to give that message to?"

"No sisters, two brothers."

"Where are you in the mix?"

"Right in the middle."

Teddy nodded. Spoiled, she judged. It rang true for middle children. Teddy was one of four siblings. She was the second child, the one who never got her way. Adam, as a middle sibling, would have always gotten his. And probably still did.

"What about you? Any brothers or sisters?" he asked.

"Two sisters, one brother."

"Do they live close by?"

Teddy shook her head. "We're pretty spread out, but we all make it home for most holidays."

"Where's home?"

"Maryland. Bentonburgh, Maryland. It's near Hagerstown, not that you've heard of either of those places."

"Actually, I have," he said.

Teddy looked at him for further explanation.

"A while ago I met a woman studying hotel management. She worked in Breezewood, the Town of Motels, for three years."

Teddy wasn't surprised he knew a woman there. She supposed he knew women in lots of places. That fact also surprisingly left her slightly cold. Deciding to move away from discussions about herself and her family, Teddy asked about him, "How did you get into investing?" He smiled at that. She recognized that type of smile. She'd seen it a hundred times on the faces of mothers or grandmothers of the brides. They were usually remembering their own weddings and knew how in love the bride was. The smile took them back in time. Adam had that look.

"My parents let me try it."

"How?"

"I had a teacher in high school who told us about the stock market. It intrigued me. It was one of the few classes I had where I sat up and listened to what he had to say." He spread his arms and hunched his shoulders. "I was fascinated by the possibility of turning a little money into a lot of it. I told my parents I wanted to try investing. They said it was too risky. That I would lose anything I had."

"And you proved them wrong," she stated.

"Very wrong, but it was a turning point."

"How?" Teddy took a sip of wine.

She gave him her full attention, just as he must have done to that high school teacher all those years ago.

"I wasn't the best kid. But in high school, who was?" He paused and gave her a long stare. "I was sixteen and rebellious. I guess I was at that age where a turn one way or the other could make me a man or send me to jail. My parents talked over the idea and agreed to let me have a thousand dollars to play with."

"Play with?" Teddy's brows rose. Her parents weren't poor, but she couldn't imagine them giving her that much money when she was in high school.

"Money was the first thing that really interested me. They would try anything that would hold my attention and keep me out of trouble," he explained. "The money was enough that I would be careful with it. So I read all the reports, learned the language, took small steps. Within a year, I'd turned the thousand into five thousand."

"You're kidding." Teddy stared at him. She knew that kind of return was unheard of.

He shook his head.

"That's a phenomenal return on investment," she said.

"It was. I made good choices and I learned that I was good with money. After that I took every class I could on investing and wealth management. After college I took a job on Wall Street, got my feet wet and struck out on my own."

He smiled, proud of himself. Teddy liked that he put his mind to something and stuck with it. "So if you're ever looking to invest..." He left the sentence hanging.

"You're not going to give me a sales pitch?"

"Why? Are you a hard sell?"

"Extremely hard," Teddy said.

"I'm good at what I do," Adam challenged.

"I see," Teddy said flatly. "So you like handling other people's money?"

"As much as you like the weddings you plan, I like building wealth."

Teddy thought about the wealth they had built, she and Diana. Both had come from humble backgrounds. Diana had been a scholarship student at Princeton, and Teddy, too, had had scholarships and had worked partially through Stanford. Both understood the need for capital and they learned management of money as a necessity to their business.

Teddy wasn't wealthy, but she was comfortable. Her designs were selling for thousands of dollars and she had a growing portfolio. It wasn't managed by Adam's company.

"What is the name of your investment firm?" Teddy asked.

"Sullivan Brothers Investment, Inc." He slipped a business card across the table to her. The ease with which he did it showed a practiced salesmanship.

Teddy had never heard of his company. That was probably a good thing. If they weren't maintaining or increasing wealth for their clients, she surely would have heard something from the many brides that came in for planning. And there was the trade show that had financial planners in attendance every year. She didn't know if his company had ever been represented.

"Your brothers are part of the business?"

He shook his head. "Initially, my brother Quinn went in with me, but quickly decided it wasn't for him. I bought him out for all of three dollars." He stopped and laughed at that.

"I suppose that laugh means you didn't actually cheat him out of a good deal?"

"He hadn't invested any capital into the setup. He did the legwork of finding the offices and his muscle in helping me buy and set up furniture. That was years ago now."

"Are you at the same location?"

He shook his head.

Weddings by Diana had moved twice. Once for a medical project, and the second time because she and Diana needed more space and they could afford a more prestigious area.

"With both of us in Princeton, I'm surprised our paths haven't crossed before," Adam said. "Of course, my hours are unpredictable when I'm dealing with overseas markets."

He gave a reason for them not seeing each other. Teddy also had an explanation. "My weekends are often taken up with weddings. And unless you attend as many as I do, we'd never meet."

"Not unless our mothers had something to do with it," he said.

The streets of Princeton were nearly deserted when Teddy and Adam left the restaurant. The September night was clear and unseasonably warm. Teddy couldn't believe they'd stayed so late. Talking to Adam had been mostly pleasant after they broke the ice and agreed that they would eat together only because they were hungry. And when she realized they wouldn't be seeing each other again, it was easier to relax.

He had a nice voice, deep and rich. It reminded her of late nights listening to "music for lovers only" on the radio. The DJs always had devastating voices that tended to reach through the woofers and grab hold of you. Teddy hadn't thought of that in a while. Mainly her radio listening was done in the car while returning from a meeting or a wedding.

Yet, Adam had that DJ kind of voice. It was reaching for her. And she was willingly leaning toward it. His breath had stirred her hair when he leaned close to her. And her own breathing became shallow and labored. Teddy's gaze dropped to his lips and she wondered what it would feel like if he kissed her. Then she snapped back, stopping herself. What was happening to her?

It was good to be outside, where the coziness of their surroundings didn't play into a fantasy world. She thought about whether she would like to see him again. Of course, she would rather he liked weddings and respected what she did, but marriage and the business of marriage wasn't for everyone. Adam had declared he was one of the ones who'd rather do without it. And that probably meant he'd rather do without her as a reminder.

"My car is parked in the lot," she said, looking behind them.

Together they turned toward the nearly deserted area. Other than their cars, she was sure the remainder belonged to the restaurant staff who were cleaning up and ready to end the night's work. Why hadn't she noticed the bar noise dying down? Or the other dinner patrons leaving? She and Adam had been engrossed in conversation, but it was the first time ever for Teddy to be so oblivious of her surroundings that she didn't realize they were alone.

Adam didn't touch her as he walked beside her to her car. Neither did he speak. She wondered what he was thinking. They could have gone on talking as long as they kept away from certain subjects, like weddings and marriage. Two that shouldn't be discussed on a first date anyway. Except this was not a date.

"Thanks for sharing my meal," he said when they stood next to her car.

Teddy thought he was being careful with his words. "I enjoyed it." It wasn't totally a lie, but it also wasn't fully the truth. She pressed the button on her key fob and heard the door unlock. As she reached for the handle, Adam called her name. She stopped. Could she have imagined the softness of his voice? She turned back.

Adam stepped closer to her. For no reason, her heartbeat accelerated. He leaned forward. Teddy leaned back an inch or so. Then his cheek brushed hers. Other than their initial handshake, this was the first time he touched her. His skin was smoothly shaven and warm. He held her for a short moment, not even long enough for her hands to reach his arms as they lifted to grasp him. Teddy didn't move. She thought he was about to hug her. Her breath caught and held, but he only reached around her to open the car door. She got in and, without a word, Adam closed the door. He stepped back and she looked up at him.

She started the car and, with a wave, pulled out of the parking space. As she reached the street, she glanced in the rearview mirror. Adam stood where she'd left him.

Color me confused, she thought.

"How was the date?" Diana asked, setting a cup of coffee on Teddy's desk.

Teddy wasn't working. Usually she would be. They had five weddings coming up in the next three months, but today her mind was on the man she'd had dinner with.

She reached for the coffee and took a sip. "He's got a dry humor. He hates weddings, doesn't believe in happily ever after, he's arrogant as hell and we won't be seeing each other again."

"That bad?"

"Right off, we agreed to shake hands and say good-bye. But it wasn't all bad. We had dinner." Teddy noticed Diana's eyebrows raise. "*Only* because we were both hungry," Teddy finished.

"What does he do?"

"He's the wizard of Wall Street. That's Wall Street in Princeton."

"Investments?"

Teddy nodded. "And he's good at it. His words, not mine. So, if we're ever ready to ditch our investments firm, I'm sure Sullivan Brothers Investments, Inc. would give us a personal presentation."

"You didn't like him even a little bit?" Diana asked.

"You know how I hate blind dates."

"I met Scott on a blind date."

Scott was Diana's husband of six months. "How you met Scott is not the same. You and he had talked to each other online for months before you decided to meet. You knew a lot about each other. Even more after you discovered you'd known each other in college. Being set up with a total stranger in a bar is not the same thing."

"Well, at least you satisfied your mother's requirement," Diana told her. "The two of you met and had dinner."

Teddy took another sip of her coffee. And they talked. Teddy thought about the night and how they had been unaware of other people around them.

"He was good-looking, though," she mumbled, almost to herself.

"Oh." Again, Diana's eyebrows rose.

Teddy blinked, bringing herself back to the office and out of the restaurant where they'd talked. "He was very direct—"

"Just like you," Diana interrupted.

"I am not direct," Teddy protested.

"Sure you're not." Sarcasm was present in her tone. "But don't get off the subject. You were saying he was good-looking…"

Teddy gave her a hard stare.

"Was he tall enough? I noticed the shoes you

changed into before you left yesterday had very high heels."

Diana knew Teddy's height requirement. "He was tall enough."

"So he was tall and good-looking. And he owns an investments company."

"And he's not The One," Teddy said, intent on ending the conversation. "Not even close."

"All right, I get it." Diana raised her hands in defeat. "Conversation over. But I have hope for you. You'll stop playing the field and find the right man one day." Diana gathered her cup and smiled. "Just like I did."

Diana headed for her office, and when Diana could no longer see her, Teddy repeated, "Not even close."

Chapter 2

Soft music played in the massive cathedral in New York. Saint Patrick's had sat on Fifth Avenue since 1858. Teddy wondered how many weddings had taken place there as she looked over the assembly of friends and relatives invited to the fourth marriage of Jessica Halston. Teddy didn't want to think about the number of favors she'd called in to make this ceremony happen. A three-time divorced non-Catholic being married at Saint Pat's. Even Cardinal Richelieu was probably turning over in his seventeenth-century grave. It was truly a miracle.

Teddy glanced around. People seated in pews spoke in low tones, but the sound rising to the high arches made even a whisper loud. Along the sides Teddy saw someone she thought she knew. She blinked. She had to be mistaken. What would Adam Sullivan be doing here? The man moved behind one of the huge columns that supported the massive structure. She waited, watching for him to reappear. Before that happened, she heard a voice through her earbud.

"The bride needs you." Renee, one of her consultants and Teddy's right hand, spoke in her ear. She pressed the earpiece closer and lowered her head to hear over the noise made by the many tourists admiring the massive building. "Where is she?"

"Dressing room."

Teddy was already moving, forgetting the man she was following. "Is she all right?" Many brides got cold feet even this close to saying "I do." It didn't matter if the bride had already been to the altar three times, she could still be plagued by reservations.

"She needs a little encouragement."

That could mean anything from a full-blown refusal to leave the dressing room, to a broken nail. Teddy moved down the stairs to the dressing room, going as fast as she could. She knocked quietly and entered. Jessica stood in the middle of the room—alone. For a fourth wedding, she looked as fresh and bright as she had at her first. Teddy had been present for all three of them.

"You look great," Teddy said. It was always good to let the bride know that her appearance was perfect. "When Donald sees you, he'll be bowled over." Teddy moved closer to her. "Would you like me to get the veil?"

"Is everything ready?" Jessica asked.

Teddy recognized the unspoken question. Most

brides had the same fear. They were afraid of being left standing at the altar. Even making the trip down the aisle for the fourth time, the fear was still there. Teddy understood how to answer her, so Jessica could conceal her fear and save face.

"Everything is ready. The bridesmaids are all here, dressed and looking like a picture. The best man and groom are in the vestibule. He's got cold hands by the way."

Jessica laughed. "Cold hands, warm feet."

Teddy felt her relax. Some of the tension left her body. Teddy lifted her veil and brought it to her. "The church is packed. Everyone is in place. All we need is you." She gave Jessica a reassuring smile. "Ready?"

"Ready."

Saint Patrick's Cathedral did not stop the tourists from walking around while services were in progress. When the strangers realized there was a wedding, they lowered their voices but did not leave the building as good manners dictated. Teddy, sitting on the last pew next to Renee, had long since relegated them to an inconsequential nuisance.

She surveyed the party in the front of the church, smiling at the perfect photo they made. Teddy's mind, however, was on the minister. Not a priest, but the result of calling in another favor. No matter how many times she heard the wedding vows, they still commanded her attention. From the corner of her eye, she saw several people moving along the outside aisle that led to the exit. A man stepped into the pew she and the three junior consultants sat on, but she wasn't looking at him. Her attention was on the bride and groom, and she thought he was being courteous to other visitors coming in the building. But when he stopped directly next to her, she turned to glance at him.

"Adam?" she whispered. "What are you doing here?"

Stunned, Teddy was so focused on Adam's unexpected appearance that she missed the last words of the ceremony and the kiss. The sudden sound of organ music snapped her out of her trance. She had to move. Adam didn't have a chance to answer her question before she was needed to take care of more details. The three consultants were all on their feet and moving outside. The bride and groom were on their way up the long aisle preceded by a photographer and a videographer. Teddy lost sight of Adam as she followed them, all the while speaking into the headset she wore.

Bright sunlight blinded her. Using one hand to shade her eyes, Teddy directed the security staff she'd hired. They were already in place controlling the crowd of well-wishers and onlookers. Teddy and her assistants helped to place the wedding party for the photographs. Adam Sullivan came into view and the two shared a moment of staring at each other before she turned back to her charges.

It wasn't like they found each other across a crowded room, she told herself. And what was he doing here, anyway? She'd seen the guest list. He wasn't on it. She had a job to do and she didn't need him here as a distraction. Jessica wanted everything to go smoothly and

Teddy prided herself on giving the bride her due. One of the security guards tapped Adam on the shoulder and he moved to the back of the crowd.

For forty minutes the photographers took pictures. Teddy held flowers, smoothed hair away from a face, pushed a bridesmaid's errant bra strap into place and even stood completely concealed behind a bridesmaid as she held the woman's dress in place for a better fit. As she did this, Teddy searched the faces on the sidelines for Adam's.

When they moved inside, Teddy stayed with the bridal party while the others headed for the reception at the Waldorf Astoria. The photographer had things under control and one of his assistants had put the items not needed on a pew. He was likely to be another forty-five minutes before finishing his capture of this moment in time. Teddy took the moment to look around for Adam.

He stood along the rear wall. She headed for him. "Your presence here can't be a coincidence," Teddy said when she was close enough to him that no one else would hear her.

"Apparently, I'm here for you."

"Me?" She frowned, her hand going to her breasts. "Why? I'm in the middle of a wedding and I didn't…I mean, we didn't agree to meet again."

"It's out of our hands."

"I don't understand," Teddy said.

"You have to pick up something this afternoon before you go back to New Jersey."

"A painting," she said. "My moth—" Teddy suddenly stopped. She fully understood. Her mother had called Adam and told him she was going to the gallery today to pick up a painting and bring it back to Princeton. When she went home in a few weeks, she'd take it with her.

"Another setup, I see," Adam said.

"You don't have to do this," Teddy protested. "I'm sure you're busy. It's a small canvas and I can carry it on the train."

"I'm here now. I don't mind driving you since we will be heading in the same direction."

"You drove?"

He nodded.

"Teddy?"

She looked back at the photographer and waved at him to indicate she'd be a moment.

"I have to go now. The reception is at the Waldorf. When I leave there I'm going—"

"I know," he interrupted. "I have all the details."

"Of course you do." Teddy knew her mother was nothing if not thorough.

"I'll see you at the reception."

Teddy nodded and rushed to the front of the church. As she went to work on the necessary details that needed attention, she couldn't help but look over her shoulder to see if Adam was still standing there.

He wasn't.

Two hours later Adam caught up with Teddy just inside the main ballroom. "Would you like to dance?" he asked.

"I'm not a guest here," she told him. "And neither are you."

"Your duties are over. You were invited to the reception, so you're free now." He took her hand and pulled her close. "Would you like to dance?"

He didn't give her time to answer. And he didn't put her hand on his waist. Her hand rested below his belt on the strong haunches of his lower back. She didn't move it—not away at least. He felt her hesitation and she pushed it down an inch. Heat rushed through his clothes, up his back and into his neck. Adam felt the scorching flame beneath her skin.

His eyes were staring at her. He had to move, snap out of the paralytic state he was in. Moving his feet, he circled her onto the floor and she fell in step with him. He knew she wouldn't fight him. That would cause a scene, and at a wedding this important or even one that wasn't, Teddy wouldn't ruin the day for the newly married couple. He'd garnered that from talking to her during their blind date.

She danced well. She was light in his arms as he led her from one step to another. She followed him as if they'd practiced for hours. Adam enjoyed it. He didn't dance much, but in his youth he'd been known to command the floor.

When the music stopped, they headed toward the staff table. Adam grabbed two bottles of water and they both drank thirstily.

"You two looked great out there." Renee smiled as she joined them. She was shorter than Teddy with light brown eyes and hair the same color that was pulled back, exposing her entire oval-shaped face.

"Adam, this is Renee Hart. She's a fantastic assistant."

Renee blushed as the two shook hands and exchanged the customary greeting. The assistant began clearing away the few things on the table that he assumed would go back to the office. Turning to Teddy, she said, "Your bag is over there." She pointed toward the wall behind the table. Adam saw a small canvas bag lying there. "We're all packed and about to head back."

"All right," Teddy said. "I'll see you on Monday."

Renee said goodbye, leaving the two of them alone.

Teddy turned back to him. "I'm finished now. I guess we should go get the painting, unless you want to dance again."

Adam drove the SUV expertly through the crowded Manhattan streets. Yellow cabs, buses and New York drivers proved no match for his skill.

"How was the wedding?" he asked.

"Do you really want to know?" Teddy remembered his comment on weddings in general. "I thought you didn't go in for the happily ever after."

"I don't. I was only making conversation."

It was a long ride back to Princeton. It would be even longer if they didn't talk. "The wedding was beautiful. The bride was beautiful. Several of her bridesmaids cried. You saw the church."

"How long does it take to plan a wedding?"

"I thought you were married before. How long did yours take?"

"We didn't have all the bells and whistles. We went to the justice of the peace and got married," Adam said.

Teddy was surprised. "Your wife didn't want a big wedding?"

"She did, but we couldn't afford it. So we decided to use the money we had for the honeymoon."

"Maybe next time," Teddy said, forgetting his beliefs.

"There will be no next time," he said. His voice was final.

"Then you better stop your mother from setting up blind dates for you."

"Oh, it's on the top of my list of things to do."

Teddy laughed. "If you find a solution to that, please send me an email and share it so I can stop my mother."

Teddy reached down and opened the small package she'd brought with her. Inside was a pair of shoes, which she traded for the ones she was wearing.

Adam glanced at her.

"Different muscles," she explained.

"What does that mean?"

"After a wedding or a long day on my feet, changing my shoes means I use different muscles in my legs and they don't get as tired."

"From the way you were all over the place, you must be tired of running."

Teddy sighed. "This one wasn't that bad. The cathedral was huge, but everything ran rather smoothly. Jessica will be pleased."

"Jessica is the bride, I take it?"

Teddy nodded. "For the fourth time."

"Four husbands?" he said.

"She keeps us in business."

He must have mulled that over. Adam lapsed into silence while he maneuvered through the traffic. Teddy realized she'd given him more ammunition to support his impression about weddings and marriage. Thankfully, traffic was clogging and Adam kept his attention on the road.

Finally they reached the gallery. Adam pulled into a space someone vacated and the two of them went inside. The place was bright with light. Huge windows covered the entire first story. Interior lights were placed strategically toward paintings to give them the best appearance.

A man came from the back of the small building. He was about six feet tall with gray hair, a potbelly and a welcoming smile. "Ms. Granville?"

Teddy nodded.

"I'm Gene Restonson, the gallery owner."

"I'm Theresa Granville, Gemma Granville's daughter, here to pick up a painting you're holding for her." Teddy introduced Adam. Gene shook hands with them both.

"We were just finishing packing it up. Give me a moment," he said with a smile that took in both her and Adam. "Excuse me."

Teddy nodded and he left them to go to the back.

The huge windows looked out on the afternoon traffic. Teddy moved away from them, going to a painting on a back wall. It was a landscape of the sea and sky. Adam came up behind her. "You know what they're doing, right?"

She turned to him. "'They'?"

"Our mothers."

"What?"

"They're going to keep throwing us together in hopes that we finally decide to date."

"I'm sure I can handle that," Teddy told him.

"I can, too. We're both very busy, but I think there's another option that will satisfy us all."

Teddy was intrigued. "What is that? You're not going to propose?" She held her breath. It wasn't possible, but she was unsure of what he might do. He'd appeared out of the blue today and after their conversation on weddings at dinner, he could be setting her up for anything.

He shook his head. "No, that's not it."

"You have my attention. What do you think we should do?"

"I think we should give them what they want."

"I thought you weren't going to propose." Teddy had no idea where this was going. "They want us to fall in love and get married."

"So we pretend to fall in love," Adam said.

"What?"

"It's not so strange."

"Pretend lovers. Those plots don't work in books, let alone with two people who don't know each other."

"That's what makes it perfect. We can spend the

time getting to know each other. At least, that's what we'll tell them."

"And how do we get out of this, when my mother starts making appointments for the church, the cake and asking me for the wedding gown design?"

"It won't go that far. We'll keep it up until Christmas. Then we'll tell them it didn't work out and we'll be free of each other."

Teddy stared at him. "Free of each other," she repeated.

"I didn't mean that the way it sounded. We'll have satisfied our parents for the time being. Mine will usually not bother me for a year after a breakup."

"And with the new year," Teddy said. "They'll be too busy to bother us for several more months. By then, maybe we can convince them that their meddling produced disastrous results and we're in command of our own love lives."

"Giving each of us time to find our own partners, if that's our intention."

Teddy shook her head, indicating that was not her intention.

"We'll call it the Marriage Pact," Adam suggested.

Teddy glanced up at him skeptically. "You know, you're way too into this."

He smiled, showing his even, white teeth.

"Shouldn't it be the Pretend We're Falling in Love Pact? After all there will be no wedding planning."

"Too many words." He frowned as if he was seriously considering it. "Are you in?"

"I'm not sure..." She hesitated. "I hate to deceive my mother." She paused a moment. "Although..."

"Although what?"

"Although she'd deceived me a number of times." Teddy remembered when her mother threatened to send out wedding invitations with "Groom: TBA" on them if Teddy didn't find her own date.

"Well?" he prompted.

"I think we should think this through more. For example, we don't know much about each other."

"We'll go on a few dates and come up with our story."

"How are we going to handle the holidays? You said this would be over by Christmas. A lot of planning goes into the family holidays."

"We'll have everything in order," he told her.

"All right," she said on a sigh. "Conditions." Teddy wasn't convinced this would work, but she'd give it a try if it had the possibility of giving her a few free months from her mother's relentless pestering.

"What conditions?"

"We go on these dates and we talk about the implications of this approach. We think this through."

"Agreed," he said.

Teddy believed he wasn't really thinking it through. "I mean, with the same consideration you give to your investments, you give to this plan."

He took a moment to consider it. Then he nodded and said, "Will do."

"Here it is," Mr. Restonson said.

Teddy turned. The gallery owner was a few feet behind her. She'd nearly forgotten about him in light of Adam's plan. She wondered if he'd heard them.

Moving across the floor, Teddy met him in the middle of the room. "It's huge," she said when she saw him carrying a package longer than her arms. The painting had been wrapped and she couldn't tell what the picture was, but she could see its size. No way could she take that on the train back to Princeton.

And her mother knew it.

Chapter 3

Adam wrestled the painting into the back of the SUV as Teddy watched. Several times she jerked her hand to help catch the falling canvas. "I apologize," she told him when they'd managed to get it in without a mishap. "Mom said it was a small painting."

"Relative term," he replied. "Compared with the murals at Times Square…" He left the sentence open, but Teddy knew what he meant. The advertisements in that area of Manhattan were described by the number of stories they covered. The smallest one she could think of was about ten-stories high.

There was that dry humor again. Teddy didn't mind it. In fact, she found it likable. They climbed into the plush cabin and Adam started the engine. He pulled into the afternoon traffic. Teddy thought about the suggestion Adam had brought up in the brightness of the gallery.

"Thinking about my proposal?" Adam broke into her thoughts.

"It isn't a proposal, not by my definition. But it is on my mind," Teddy said. She lapsed into silence. She knew he was waiting for her to continue by the way he glanced at her.

"Afraid pulling it off might be an issue?"

"Aren't you? After all, these are *our* parents. And what about girlfriends? I can't imagine you don't already have one." He had met her for a blind date. That should indicate that he was unattached, but Teddy didn't want to assume. She noticed him stiffen. Hands that had been relaxed now gripped the steering wheel harder.

"I did," he said quietly. "We broke up six months ago."

Teddy intentionally kept her voice low. "Is it over or do you think you'll reconcile?"

"No reconciliation." The note in his voice was final, even if it was a little higher pitched than she remembered. Teddy knew that wasn't the end of it, but she didn't know him well enough to continue questioning.

"What about you? Beautiful, confident, business owner. There must be a man in the wings."

"Several," Teddy said.

"Anyone in particular?"

"They're all particular."

He took his eyes from the road to stare at her with raised eyebrows. "How many is 'all'?"

"Not a relevant question, or one I'll answer," she told him.

"So the Marriage Pact won't work for you?"

"I didn't say that," Teddy said, a teasing smile curving her lips.

"What are you saying?"

"I'm not sure. There are complications that could happen from this action and I don't know what they are yet."

"Does that mean you'll think about it?"

After a long moment, she said, "I'll think about it."

They were both quiet for the rest of the drive. When they entered the Borough of Princeton, Teddy directed him to her house.

"Where do you want it?" Adam asked, carrying the painting.

"In here, slide it between the columns." She led him to the area between her living and dining rooms. They were separated by a pair of columns. Teddy pointed to a spot that didn't obstruct her entry or exit. Adam leaned the painting against the wall and followed her back to the kitchen.

"Would you like something to drink?" she asked.

"Thank you, but I need to go. Japanese markets are open and I have some transactions to take care of."

"Of course," Teddy said. She was slightly disappointed that he wasn't staying. She headed back toward the front of the house. At the door, she turned to thank him for his help, but a sudden and unexpected emotion gripped her. She looked up at him. The idea of a pretense with him wasn't sitting as badly as it should.

Her eyes roamed his face, settling on his mouth. Teddy thought of leaning toward him but stopped herself.

"Is something wrong?" he asked.

She shook her head.

"You will think about the pact?" he asked.

Teddy nodded. "I promised." Then surprised herself by adding, "We could talk more about it sometime." She hesitated and that was unlike her. "After the markets close, maybe."

"We need to know more about each other," he agreed.

She nodded.

"While you're thinking, here's something to help you along."

Before Teddy knew what he was going to do, he leaned toward her and she couldn't help but lean into him. Her head tipped up and her heels came off the floor at the same time. His mouth hovered over hers. He took her face in his hands, first one hand, then the other, cradling her. She took in his scent. Images swam before her eyes. She closed them as emotions burned within her. Intense heat flashed through her until she was sure she was glowing yellow. His mouth settled on hers. Easy. He didn't rush or plunge. His fingers threaded through her hair, combing it with ease as if he savored the texture and feel of the dark strands. Palms slid across her shoulders and with slow, caressing movements skimmed over her arms and sides before wrapping around her waist. He pulled her against him, possessively, his mouth mirroring the actions of his body. She felt the fire of his hands searing her suit fabric.

Teddy had been kissed before, but never like this, never with this tenderness, this softness that was as unnerving as if he were devouring her. Her arms reached upward, sliding over arms that were rock hard. On tiptoe she circled his neck and pressed herself into him. Just as her mouth began to mate with his, he lifted his head.

She said nothing. Her eyes closed and opened in answer. His finger on her lips made her incapable of speech. The emotions rifling through her were new, untried, outside her realm of experience. But they were there—prickling electrical points that dotted her body, vibrated over her skin like a formfitting acupuncture machine that dealt only in pleasure. The sensation was new.

Adam moved his hand and the moment snapped, a tenuous thread broken.

"Now we know what it's like to kiss each other."

Reaching around her, he opened the door. She was already close enough to him that the smell of his heady cologne clouded her senses. Brushing against his hard body as she made room for him had her responding to the pure sexual drive of him.

The door clicked shut and she let out a long breath. She was incapable of speech. When had a man ever caused her to react like this?

And one her mother *handpicked!*

Teddy understood that if she agreed to Adam's suggestion, the two should keep it secret, but she told Diana everything. In this she needed a second opinion.

"So, what do you think?" Teddy asked as she finished explaining Adam showing up at the wedding, the painting and his suggestion. She omitted the devastating kiss at her front door.

Diana stared at her with openmouthed amazement. "He suggested you pretend to be in love?"

Hearing it put like that and in a tone that said it was incredible, Teddy was sorry she'd brought up the subject.

"Do you think it will work?" Diana asked.

"I'm not sure. I'd rather just tell my mother to back off, but we both know that won't work."

Diana leaned forward, her arms folded on her desk. "Let me ask a different question. Are you considering this because you're attracted to Adam?" Teddy hesitated. It was apparently too long for Diana. "I guess that's my answer."

"I told you he was good-looking." Actually he was gorgeous. He had the most amazing eyes, light brown with a fringe of lashes that any female would be jealous of. His hands were soft when he had them on her face, but she could feel the strength in them. His body was solid and that bedroom voice could possibly undo her.

"At the time you didn't say you wanted to spend time with him. What is this, your third date?" Diana asked.

"We haven't been on a date yet."

"What was dinner last week and the wedding on Friday?"

"Those were chance meetings."

Diana frowned at her, but her face showed the opposite. "Sure they were," she said sarcastically. "But as far as your question goes, you'll have to decide. If you're doing it to ward off your mom, that's one thing. But if you just want to spend time with the guy and he with you, I'm sure neither one of you needs a guise."

Teddy thought about that. She was confused about her reasons for considering the Marriage Pact. She'd never wanted to be married in the past. Even though she loved the planning of someone else's wedding, she'd never thought of doing it for herself. So Adam should be a perfect candidate in her life. He didn't like weddings, didn't want to have anything to do with happily ever after. So why didn't Teddy just take him up on the Marriage Pact and fall in with his plans? It would make everyone happy. Did she really want to continue seeing Adam? Granted, if she'd met him on her own, she'd have no problem going out with him. But in her usual manner, as Diana put it, Teddy would quickly move on to someone else.

There was a certain chemistry between them. Teddy felt it. Her mouth tingled just thinking about the kiss the two of them had shared. Was that the reason? Was she afraid of spending time with him? They could become close. Was that so bad? Diana and Scott hadn't begun on the best foot and they were happily married now. Was Teddy protecting herself, putting up barriers to prevent her life from changing?

Neither she nor Adam really needed to fall in with their parents' wishes. She was her own woman, with her own needs and plans. So why was she so undecided about Adam?

* * *

Adam stared at himself in his bedroom mirror. Who was this guy, he mentally asked himself? He'd never acted this way before. He liked Teddy. He really liked her. And that was his problem. He *really* liked her. In fact, he felt as if his feelings were morphing into something else, something more. It didn't make any sense. If there had been a lineup of beautiful women before him, Adam would never have selected her as someone he wanted to get to know, but he did want to know her.

Grabbing a sweater from the drawer, he shrugged into it, dropping the one he'd spilled beer on in the hamper. Then he went into the kitchen and popped the top off another can of beer. Joining his brother in front of the big-screen television in his family room, he dropped down next to him and tossed him a can.

There was a baseball game on ESPN and Quinn was watching it. The moment he arrived, he went straight for the TV and turned on the game. When Adam joined him, he took his eyes away from the screen for a moment. Quinn was the athletic brother. He not only watched every sporting event possible, but in high school and college, he played baseball and tennis, and competed in track. He was still active in tennis and jogged several miles a day. Adam didn't envy him his biceps. Adam had his own workout routine that could rival his brother's.

Adam knew Quinn had been observing him closely for the past few days. He didn't think he'd changed since he and Teddy talked about their Marriage Pact, but he knew his observant brother must have noticed a change in him. Anything that removed Quinn's attention from a game in progress had to be important.

"What are you thinking?" Adam asked.

"That something is wrong with you."

"I'm fine," Adam said.

"Since Mom fixed you up with that blind date, you haven't been the same."

"Which blind date? There have been several. Often I can get out of them." Adam knew the routine with his mother. She would call, pretend to ask him something about investing or going through some amount of small talk, before mentioning that she'd run in to so-and-so from his past or that she'd met a very nice woman who was unattached and who would like to meet him.

Other than giving her an out-and-out no, which he'd done on one occasion, he put them off by telling her he already had a date. Sometimes that was true. Sometimes he then found a date to make the lie come true.

"You know which date," Quinn said. "The one you had a few weeks ago."

Adam took a sip of beer. "How have I been different?"

"You're quieter."

"Aren't you the one who's always telling me to be quiet so you can hear the television?" Adam said, glancing at the TV screen, and sipped his beer to cover the uncomfortable feeling that washed over him.

"I never thought you'd actually do it."

"I'm getting older…and wiser."

"Nope," Quinn said.

"Nope?"

"You're getting older, but I think we can thank Ms. Theresa Granville for the change."

Adam stiffened. "She has nothing to do with this."

"Not what I heard."

"What do you mean?" Adam frowned. "What have you heard? And from whom?"

"I mean, the word is that the two of you are a couple."

"Yeah?"

"It's true." A commercial came on and Quinn hit the mute button on the remote control. He turned to Adam. "Someone's gotten under your skin?"

Adam understood what Teddy meant by not truly thinking through the deception angle. He'd intended to fend off his mother. He hadn't thought that he'd have to keep the pretense up with everyone else, including his brothers. But the fewer people who knew the truth, the better. And while Quinn could keep a secret, Adam decided it wasn't the time to reveal what he and Teddy had talked about.

"It had to happen sometime," he answered Quinn. Adam hated lying to his brother, but if their deception was to work, only the two of them could know about it. And Adam was confused by Teddy. She seemed to tap into something deep inside him and he was unsure of what it was. Keeping it under wraps was the right thing to do, he told himself.

"This from the man who said falling in love wasn't for him. That he intended to play the field the rest of his life. Then you meet Veronica." Quinn paused, giving Adam a long look. "Then that didn't work out and you find Teddy. Two out of two. Or is Teddy a re-bound love?"

"Teddy is nothing like Veronica."

"Is she more like Chloe?"

Adam tensed. His brother knew better than to bring up Chloe. But Adam didn't want to let on that her name disturbed him. Chelsea, who he parted with on a mutually friendly basis, was never the subject of their man-woman discussions. But she had an impact on his life as did the other women. Chloe was a different story.

"She's nothing like Chloe," he said. He hadn't compared them, but Teddy was her own person. Maybe that was why he couldn't identify her. Adam thought of their kiss. For days afterward, he couldn't get the feel of her in his arms out of his mind. He liked the way her body folded into his as if she belonged there. As if she wanted to be there. As if it was the right place for her. And he wanted nothing more than to go on holding her.

In the time since he decided to never marry again, he hadn't met anyone who captured his mind days after meeting the way Teddy had. Pushing himself up straight on the sofa, Adam became very serious. He scrutinized Quinn for a moment before asking, "Have you ever been in love? I mean, really in love? Have you ever wanted a woman more than you've wanted anything else?"

Quinn pointed the remote control at the television and clicked it off. "This is going to take some time."

For a long moment Quinn stared at Adam. The two brothers were close and rarely held anything from each other. Adam wanted to tell him about the pact, but not yet.

"You think you're in love?" Quinn asked, breaking Adam's train of thought.

"No."

"Then what *do* you think?"

"I'm not sure. I think I might be going through some kind of phase."

"Phase?" Quinn grunted. "You're way too old for phases."

"Has it happened to you, Quinn?" Adam asked seriously.

His brother hesitated. Then said, "Once."

"With who? What happened? Why didn't I know about this?"

"You have your own life and mainly you work after dark."

"I work with world markets. They're open late," Adam said. "What about the woman you were in love with?"

"Obviously it wasn't the can't-live-without-you love, since I am still here. And this conversation is not about me," Quinn countered. "Does Mom have anything to do with this?"

"Not much. She's always meddling in my love life."

"Well, you haven't been seeing anyone on a steady basis," Quinn said. "And that's a cue for her to take control."

"So she finds me dates. Blind dates."

Quinn smiled. "So that's what this is about. She got you a date and you're having feelings for her."

"Not totally. I mean, Teddy is a nice person. I'd have dated her on my own if Mom hadn't interfered. But I'm not in love with her."

"What about Veronica and Chloe? Weren't you in love with them?"

"I thought I was. Veronica was all flash."

"And Chloe?"

"I'll never know."

The parking lot was nearly empty when Teddy returned from her last appointment. She usually loved it when there was a lot of activity going on, but she was in no mood to deal with overzealous mothers or brides who wanted a wedding the size of a Hollywood star on a budget that wouldn't support a B-level film. For the past three days, Teddy felt as if she'd been on a merry-go-round. She had rushed from one meeting to another, juggling details, approving orders and trying her best to put Adam out of her mind. The work was nothing compared to thoughts of Adam. The effort resulted in a headache as both sides of her brain warred with each other.

The offices of Wedding by Diana had recently moved from a scenic but cramped building in downtown Princeton to more spacious surroundings on the fringe of the township. They had a large parking lot and easy access to the major thoroughfares. The offices were brighter and much better organized, although Teddy knew that happened because they had moved and put everything in a new and neat place. Maintaining it would be a chore, but Diana was good at that.

Opening the glass double doors, Teddy balanced the bundles in her arms and headed for her office. A peal of laughter had her stopping just inside. The receptionist looked up and smiled. Teddy was used to hearing happy female voices when she returned from afternoon appointments. She wasn't used to hearing male laughter unless Diana's husband, Scott, had dropped by. This was a decidedly female domain. More laughter rang out. Her heartbeat quickened as she recognized the low masculine sound. Adam! What was he doing here? Again here he was, unannounced and throwing her emotions out of kilter.

Dropping her portfolio and packages in her office, she took a deep breath, squared her shoulders and entered Diana's office.

"Hello," Teddy said.

All conversation stopped. Adam stood up. His smile brightened when he saw her and for a moment Teddy almost forgot she was angry with him. This was her workplace and she didn't need him dropping by and confusing her. She had too many details to remember and he was somehow invading her thoughts and making it difficult for her to concentrate.

"You didn't tell me Adam was a stand-up comic," Diana said, a smile brightening her face.

Teddy looked from Diana to Adam. His humor with her hadn't been comedic.

"He's been regaling me with stories about some of his clients' questions while he waited for you."

"Sorry I'm late." Teddy acted as if she had expected him all along, which she hadn't.

Adam said goodbye to Diana and followed Teddy to her office. "Did we have an appointment that I don't know about?" she asked the moment she closed the door. "Because I don't have you on my calendar and I'm very good at keeping track of the people I'm supposed to meet."

"I couldn't wait any longer," he said.

"For what?" Teddy frowned. Confusion had to show on her face.

He took a moment to look around. Wedding portraits hung on the walls. Fabric books sat in a corner. Samples of netted veils hung from a rack near a conference table.

"To get your answer. I thought this setting might generate a positive response."

"And that's what you want?"

"I think it could benefit us both."

For some reason, Teddy thought he was referring to their kiss.

"And…my mother called," he finished. "Are you done for the day?"

The question was an abrupt change in subject and just as abruptly her heart lurched. There were a few hundred details that needed her attention, but they could wait until morning. She nodded.

"Why don't we go somewhere and talk?"

Teddy looked at the pile of bundles she'd brought in with her. Usually she would spend time organizing them. She'd check the notes she'd made during her meetings and put them in the proper files or set up her to-do list for the next day. Yet, when Adam asked about her time, her heartbeat increased. She wanted to go with him.

A moment later they said good-night to Diana, whose face hid a smirk, and left the office. Ten minutes later, they sat at a small table in a local bar where the waitress addressed Adam by name.

"Come here often?" Teddy teased when the woman left to get their drinks.

He smiled and appeared uncomfortable.

"You don't have to answer that," she said, teasing still in her voice. "This is a small town."

"I'm sure there are places where you're recognized," he told her.

"Many of them," she admitted. "My job requires it."

"Mine, too," he said. "Really," he repeated at her skeptical look. "Depending on the market, my hours can be unpredictable. Often this is the only place to get food after midnight."

"No snack bar at the company you own?"

"By midnight it's empty and I prefer more than a diet of potato chips and chocolate."

Teddy didn't reply. He reminded her of chocolate, the kind that was dark and bittersweet, but with a good measure of milk. For a moment, she wanted to taste him, see if that body had the same feel and texture of melt-in-your-mouth chocolate. Teddy had once planned a chocolate wedding. Everything from the cake to the trays that held the multiple sugary concoctions had been made of chocolate: dark chocolate, milk chocolate, white chocolate. Some with nuts. Others with designs made of dried strawberries, raspberries or blueberries. She imagined Adam fully sculptured in a rich, milky flavor that would make her teeth ache.

"White wine," the waitress said, setting a glass in front of Teddy and snapping her mental musings. She set a beer glass in front of Adam, poured the honey-colored liquid into the cooled glass and left them with a friendly smile.

Teddy sipped the dry wine.

"What's it to be?" Adam brought up the subject she'd been dreading.

"You're sure this will work?" Teddy wavered in her decision. She'd spoken to Diana, but thinking of her mother had set her pulse on edge.

"How can it fail?" Adam asked. "Going on a few harmless dates will play right into their plans."

"And the girlfriends?" Teddy asked, intentionally using the plural. "Suppose we commit to this and the one woman you want above all others walks into your life? How are you going to explain me to her? Or the change in women to your mother?"

She'd seen the expression on his face change. There was a woman in his past. The proverbial one that got away.

"That's not likely to happen," he said.

"What about me? My one and only could show up unexpectedly."

He tried to cover his surprise, but Teddy saw the eyebrow rise over his left eye before he forced it back in place.

"Is there a chance of that?" He leaned forward, cradling his beer in both hands, and spoke in a low voice.

"It could. I don't live in a convent."

He waited a moment as if he was weighing his options. He had no options. "I wouldn't hold you to the terms. I'm sure your mom would be even more pleased to know her daughter had found the *right* man."

Teddy understood the implication. *He* wasn't the right man. This wasn't going the way she expected it would. She felt as if she'd somehow hurt Adam, although she didn't know how.

"In that case," Teddy began, "knowing that a true romance with someone else can and would complicate things, we agree to end this pretense early should that happen." She stared at him. "Agreed?"

"Agreed." Adam raised his glass and clinked it with hers to seal the deal.

"So, how do we begin?" she asked.

"We've already begun."

The kiss they'd shared came to Teddy's mind. She didn't know if he was into public displays of affection, but her brides and grooms had no problem letting the world know they'd found that special someone.

"We need to get to know each other, so if our parents quiz us we'll have similar stories."

"Similar? Not the same?"

He shook his head. "When my dad tells a story, my mom is always correcting his details."

"Does that happen in reverse, too?"

"You bet it does and it's amusing to watch."

For the next two hours, over a variety of tasty appetizers, Teddy and Adam enjoyed their first date. They exchanged stories about siblings, colleges attended, pros and cons of their jobs, past jobs, foods they liked and disliked, favorite colors, pet peeves. Teddy found him extremely easy to talk to and his humor wasn't as dry as she'd originally thought it was.

As the waitress replaced Teddy's third glass of wine with a cup of coffee, Teddy brought up the subject every serious relationship couple should know about—past relationships.

"Why did you and your last girlfriend break up?"

Adam coughed and shifted in his seat. Teddy had asked her question after he finished a sip of coffee. She expected his reaction and was not disappointed. She had to stop herself from laughing at his surprise.

"Why is that relevant?"

"For several reasons," she said, leaning toward him. "It'll give me insight to your character if you're totally honest. And it'll tell me some of the pitfalls I should avoid. It can also tell me some qualities your parents will compare in me. But we'll get to parents later. Let's stick with the girlfriend for now."

Adam leaned back in his chair and crossed his arms. He wore an ecru Irish knit sweater that contrasted with the darkness of his skin. "Her name was Veronica and we weren't compatible."

"I'm sure there's more to it than those few words. And your reluctance to discuss her tells me the end of the story is still unfolding."

"It's over," he said. "We didn't really like each other. She didn't make an effort to get to know me." He paused. "She never delved into my likes or dreams the way you have in the past few hours. And you're doing it on a pretense basis. With her it was supposed to be real."

"So how did you become a couple?"

"With my hours it's hard to meet and maintain relationships. Hence, my mother." He stopped a moment to flash her a grin.

"Your mother introduced you to Veronica?"

"I met Veronica at a party given by a business colleague. She was fun, lots of laughs, beautiful. I ran into her several times randomly. One day we agreed to meet. From then on, we were a couple."

"And then you found her with another man."

Adam gasped. "How did you know?"

"I had a few clues. Your hours. The fact that you never said anything about being in love. It was either another man or you didn't meet the approval of the king. The king being her father. And since you also omitted a king, it had to be a man." Teddy gazed at him, but he said nothing. "And now you've sworn off my entire sex?"

"Something like that," he admitted.

"Veronica couldn't have been the first. But you must have felt something for her that she didn't feel for you. Something deep and fearful."

Adam cleared his throat. "Can we change the subject? I believe it's your turn now. Who's the one who got away in your past?"

"I haven't met him yet."

"And how old are you?" he asked with a humorous, skeptical eye.

"Thirty, why?"

"I know there's been someone special in your life, other than the *they're-all-special* types. Which one stood out?"

Teddy hesitated for a long moment. She knew she had to answer. Adam had answered her questions. And she was the one who opened this dialogue. It was only fair that she tell him the truth.

"We called him Chad, but his name was Charles Davis. We were high school sweethearts." She stopped, gazing at Adam, remaining quiet for a few moments. "We'd known each other since the cradle. In grammar school, when boys and girls discover we aren't the sorrowful creatures we each thought the other was, Chad and I were a couple."

Teddy smiled, remembering the good times they had.

"What happened?" Adam asked quietly.

"We stayed together all through high school. He was my date to the junior and senior proms."

"Then college came," Adam added.

Teddy nodded. Her smile was gone and the heartache she'd felt all those years ago rushed back. Not as sharp. Not as raw. But still present. Teddy guessed that until someone replaced those feelings in her, she would have this spot that wasn't filled.

"He went to Northeastern. I went to Stanford."

"Let me guess. He found someone else in college."

She shook her head. "Not in college. He did a summer internship for an international bank. He was extremely excited that he was going to spend the summer in Switzerland. That's where he met her."

"How long did it take to get over him?"

Teddy lowered her chin and looked up at him. "Is that the question you really want to ask?"

"Perception kicking in again," he admitted. "Have you ever gotten over him?"

"I think so."

"But…" he prompted.

"Diana wouldn't agree with me." Before he could ask what that meant, Teddy explained. "Diana thinks I don't date seriously because I never got over Chad."

Adam leaned in close and his voice was conspiratorially low when he spoke. "Since we're baring our hearts here, in your heart of hearts, is that the truth?"

Teddy didn't have to think about it, but she took a moment to let the question gain weight. "At first I did. After a couple of years, I discovered it was up to me to decide if I was going to let my life be determined by that one incident or if I was going to pick up the pieces and build on my abilities."

"Since college you haven't been in a serious relationship?"

"Like I said, I just haven't found the right guy." She smiled and sipped her coffee again. "And that's why my mother is on the husband-hunting warpath." Teddy laughed hoping to lighten the mood. "Was Veronica the catalyst for your mom?"

Adam shook his head. "My mom has been on the marriage path since I was old enough to date. We have a family joke, that we can see the wheels in her head turning every time one of us goes on a second date."

"I guess she's not one of those mothers keeping her sons tied to her apron strings."

Adam shook his head. "She's the kind running with scissors. Secretly, I believe she's always wanted a daughter."

Teddy wondered what his mother had thought of his ex-wife, Chelsea, and Veronica. Had she embraced them, thinking they would be her daughter-in-law? Had she dreamed that one of them would be the daughter she wanted?

Teddy wondered where she would fit in the mix. Could she fulfill those requirements? Would any woman do, or did his mother have specific requirements that she wanted in her son's wife?

"What's she going to think of me?"

Adam reached over and took Teddy's hand. "She'll be more than thrilled."

Chapter 4

Cocking her head to the side, Teddy listened. She heard the slamming of car doors. Her parents had arrived. Her mother was already rushing to the door when Teddy opened it. Grabbing Teddy and folding her into a bear hug that could break a normal person's back, her mother was genuinely happy to see her. Released, Teddy hugged her dad—not quite as exuberantly as her mother's hug. Still she was happy to see her parents.

Out of the blue, her mom called on Monday to say they were coming up midweek. Teddy had to work doubly hard to get everything in order for the weekend wedding she had on her calendar and take a day off to spend with her parents.

"This is a surprise. Did you just decide to drop by

for a visit?" Teddy asked. "Not that I'm not glad to see you." When her mom called, she didn't give any other information except they were coming up for two days and that she had to rush and finish packing.

"I'm giving a lecture," her dad said. "Apparently the main speaker for Princeton's journalism symposium is ill. They asked me to fill in."

"I'm impressed," Teddy said with a smile and a hug.

As the owner/editor of a small town newspaper, Kevin Granville found wide distribution due to his various editorials. This wasn't the first time he'd been asked by universities to speak, but it was the first time he'd be going to Princeton University. And it gave Teddy the opportunity to see her parents other than over holidays like Thanksgiving and Christmas.

"Come on in. I've made lunch," Teddy told them. "I'll help you with your luggage."

"No luggage," her mom said. "The university put us up in a hotel. We've already dropped our bags."

They entered the house and Teddy went straight to the kitchen.

"I'm not going to eat much," her mom said. "We have plans for dinner. We're going to Smithville."

This was the first time Teddy had heard anything about this. Of course, the university could be taking them out to dinner, but Smithville had to be a hundred miles south of the university town.

Over a lunch of cold salads and broiled salmon, Teddy's dad outlined his lecture. Teddy asked a lot of questions. She could tell her mother was antsy to discuss Adam, and while Teddy's interest in her father's program wasn't that strong, holding her mom's crusade at bay was both humorous and tiring.

"Teddy, not to change the conversation, but where is the painting you brought for me?" Her mother finally managed to wedge into the discussion.

"It's in the dining room." She turned to her dad. "You'll have to carry it out. It's a little larger than Mom led me to believe."

"You had Adam there to help you," Gemma Granville said. "I didn't think you'd have a problem."

There it was, Teddy thought. She'd gotten Adam's name into the conversation. This was the opportunity she'd been waiting for. And there'd be no stopping her probe for details.

"Thanks to you and his mother." Teddy glanced at her mom, giving her that stop-interfering look. But Gemma just smiled.

To her husband, she said, "Kevin, would you get it and put it in the car?"

The look her father gave her mother was one Teddy had seen many times. He knew she was on a crusade and whatever his efforts, she wouldn't be derailed.

"It's between the columns," Teddy directed.

Alone with her mom, Teddy took her favorite mug from the cabinet and one for her mom. She filled them with coffee and returned to the table.

"I was surprised Adam wasn't with you," her mother said as she sipped the hot liquid.

"It's his parents' anniversary and he's having a dinner for them."

"Oh, he didn't invite you?"

"Mom," she warned. "We're not joined at the hip."

"Not yet," her mother whispered. Teddy didn't think she was supposed to hear that. At least she gave her mom the benefit of the doubt.

"I do like him," Teddy said, sipping from the mug and beginning her subterfuge.

Her mom smiled. "Do you think he might be The One?"

The hopeful lift to her voice made Teddy feel guilty. She hated deception, but she'd agreed to this fake proposal so she had to go through with it.

"I'm not sure," she said. "But we're going to keep seeing each other. Wherever it goes, it goes."

"That's a start."

She patted her daughter's hand the same way she had when Teddy was a gawky teenager in need of her motherly advice.

"Mom, don't get your hopes up. This may not work out. We've met a couple of times."

"But you agreed to another date," her mother stated.

Teddy nodded. "We liked each other enough to try it."

"Good." Her mother clasped her hands together.

"Stop," Teddy said. "You'll get excited about this and it could be over in a matter of weeks." Teddy knew it would be over in a short time period. She and Adam had already set their expiration date.

"Oh, don't be so negative," her mother said. "He could be the best thing that happened to you. Give it some time." After another sip of her coffee, she said,

"Speaking of dinner, you're invited so I hope you have something dressy to wear. I mean, something special."

They hadn't been discussing dinner, but it was a safer subject than Adam, so Teddy let the change happen. Of course she had a nice dress. Her mother knew Teddy had a closet full of clothes for every occasion. Yet she felt Teddy needed to make an impression on someone who would be attending the dinner, someone who could probably help her father. She wondered what her mother was wearing. "The university must be going all out for Dad."

"Oh, they are."

Teddy found out why she needed the *special* dress several hours later when her father pulled into the parking lot of a restaurant too many miles from home for Teddy not to be suspicious.

"This is a really long way from Princeton," Teddy commented as they exited the car.

"I hear the food is good," her mom said. "Have you been here before?"

"I've done a couple of weddings here. And the food *is* really good."

"It's beautiful." Her mom took a moment to look at the small village. Every shop was completely outlined in tiny white lights. Teddy knew the area was lighted this way year-round.

"If you ever do your own wedding, you can probably use this as a place for a reception."

Her mother's message wasn't lost on Teddy. She ignored it and looked at the building. The place was huge and it had a large parking lot. When you lived in Princeton, you understood the need for adequate parking since it was at a premium in the college town.

Inside the place was warm and inviting. She didn't hear her father give his name, but they bypassed all the people in the waiting area and followed the receptionist to an adjacent room.

All Teddy's training and experience at remaining calm and keeping her emotions in check deserted her when she entered the private party room. She gasped. Adam sat at a U-shaped table with people who were obviously his parents. She assumed the others were his brothers and their dates. He'd told her neither of his siblings were married.

Adam stood up slowly and stared at her. "Wow," he said, taking a long moment to look her up and down. Teddy felt a blush cover her, but couldn't deny that she liked the way he made her feel. Now she understood why her mother insisted on checking to see what she was wearing. The black knee-length sequined dress lay haphazardly on her closet floor where it had fallen when her mother rejected it for the scarlet strapless chiffon she now wore.

Disengaging himself from the group, Adam came to stand in front of their three-person party. He kissed her lightly on the lips. "I don't know what's going on," he whispered. Then in a louder voice, he said, "Let me take your coat," as if he'd been expecting her. She handed him the drape she had over her arm and he placed it on an unoccupied chair at an empty table. Apparently, the assembled party of guests were the only occupants of the room.

Teddy introduced her parents. Behind him Adam's mother and father had risen and now stood in front of her. Adam introduced Merle Sullivan and Dr. Ann Sullivan, and Teddy already suspected her mother knew Adam's mom. Adam's father was the CEO of a mid-size insurance company. He was a portly man, over six feet tall with thinning hair that was a mixture of gray and black. Dr. Sullivan was short and petite. Her hair was cut almost to her scalp, making her face strong and prominent. Yet her smile was beautiful and Adam had gotten his eyes from her. Teddy didn't have time to process all the information because the other family members quickly joined the small congregation. Galen and Quinn were Adam's brothers. Both had dates and Teddy wondered if they were also on the receiving end of their mother's quest for married sons.

Adam slipped his arm around her waist and she felt heat flow to her toes. As everyone headed for the table to retake their seats, Adam took her hand. The two lingered behind the others, staying close to the entrance.

"It wasn't my idea. I nearly swallowed my teeth when the three of you walked in," he said. He stopped and glanced over his shoulder. "But I can see my mother's hand in this…coincidence."

"Well, I suppose it's time we went into our act," she said, her voice low. "Get ready."

"For what?"

"The *Gemma Granville Marry My Daughter Show*."

Adam almost laughed at that. Teddy had no way of knowing that his mother could hold her own when it came to her sons and the marriages that were still to come. Quinn and Galen weren't immune to their mother's machinations, but tonight they weren't on the front line.

Glancing at Quinn, Adam noticed the shadow of a smile on his brother's face. He could almost hear him asking, *Is she the one?* Adam had no answer for that. There was something indefinable about Teddy, but so far the two were only trying to solve the problem between themselves and their overzealous mothers.

"Are you two going to hover over there all night or join the rest of us?" Quinn called from his place across the room.

Adam and Teddy turned to face Quinn and the waiting table. Adam put his hand on her back and urged her toward the U-shaped table that had been laid out festively for an anniversary. Both the chairs and tables had been covered in white. Place settings were laid out for a six-course meal. Adam wasn't sure he'd survive it.

The two took seats. "Sorry for holding things up," Teddy apologized to Adam's parents.

"Don't worry about it." His mother brushed her apology aside. She placed a hand on her husband's and continued. "We remember how it was to be newly in love."

Adam's ears should have slid off his face at the amount of heat that flashed within him so fast the entire room had to see it. Glancing at Teddy, he was surprised to see her smiling.

"You think this is funny?" he whispered.

"Hilarious." Then she gave her attention to his parents. "Adam didn't tell me how long you've been married."

"Tonight we celebrate thirty-eight years," his father responded for the first time since their introduction. He smiled, one Adam had seen many times and knew was genuine.

"Happy years." Quinn raised his glass and toasted them.

"Can you imagine being married that long, Teddy?" her mother asked.

"Mother, I can't imagine being married for one year, let alone several decades. But…" She paused and took Adam's hand. Hers was warm and calm, while his, despite the heat generating in his body, was ice-cold. He wondered where she was going with this. "…maybe one day we'll all meet again for an anniversary and I'll answer that question."

Adam thought his mother was going to beam out of her chair. The smile on her face rivaled the size of her dinner plate. Quinn looked stunned. His brother Galen's mouth dropped open and Teddy's mother's face mirrored that of her coconspirator.

"Wait a minute," Galen said. "Are you telling me, you two are serious?" He pointed from one to the other with the index fingers of both hands.

Adam cleared his throat. "Well, we haven't known each other that long, but…" he stopped for effect and the need to swallow the lump of lies he was about to tell "…things are progressing."

"Progressing?" Galen repeated.

Teddy nodded. "I hope you have no objections." She gazed directly at Galen, then turned to his parents.

Adam's mom spread her hands. "We're thrilled." Then a moment later, she continued, "Of course, we want you two to be sure."

Adam watched the bobbing heads. He knew the two mothers in this room had already decided that they were more than sure.

Teddy held her sides, hesitating on the steps to her porch, as she laughed for the hundredth time during their ninety-minute drive back to Princeton. She and Adam had reviewed the evening's events since leaving the restaurant and climbing into his car. Adam drove and Teddy was glad she didn't have to negotiate the dark roads as tears sometimes trickled down her cheeks over some comment or action one or both of their mothers had made.

She opened the door to her house and both entered the dimly lit foyer.

"If you don't stop," she informed Adam, "I'm going to have to go to the hospital so they can stitch up my sides." She took short breaths, trying to control the pain in her sides, but she started to laugh again. Hiccupping, she stopped.

"I apologize for my parents," she told him after a moment.

"It was just as much my mother's fault as yours."

"They ambushed us."

"But we were ready. I'm sure both of them went home as happy souls."

He smiled at Teddy and it was almost her undoing. Every time she saw him, her heart fluttered and her stomach felt as if butterflies were playing inside her.

"Do you want something to eat?"

"I'm starving," he said. "I couldn't eat anything during dinner."

"I know." Teddy headed for the kitchen. "Between your brothers and our parents, I was afraid I'd choke if I tried to swallow anything."

Teddy started to laugh again. Tears cornered in her eyes and she used her fingertips to wipe them away.

"Quinn." She paused, taking a sobering breath. "When Quinn asked your mom where she was hiding my wedding gown and the room went deathly quiet, I thought she might answer that it was in the coat closet."

Adam laughed. "Then Galen joined with…" He stopped as they both remembered his brother coming up with the same thought about where the gown was located. "And then adding that the minister was probably coming in for dessert and would perform the nuptials."

"The look on your mom's face was priceless, even though I was totally afraid my mother might say it was all true," Teddy said.

The gales of laughter continued. Teddy held her head. All the laughing was making it throb. She forced herself to control it and went into the kitchen.

Adam followed her. "Can I help with anything?" he asked as she opened the refrigerator.

Teddy stopped and stared at him. "Can you cook?" she asked.

"I've been known to boil water," he said. "And I

make a mean macaroni and cheese. If pushed, I can boil spaghetti and open a jar of sauce."

Teddy smiled. "I'm not used to having anyone in my kitchen, so why don't you set the table?" She pointed to the cabinets holding plates, glasses and silverware. "Does your mother also find dates for your brothers?" Teddy asked.

"Often," he said. "They threatened to accept jobs far from home if she didn't stop."

"And that worked?" It seemed an easy solution. Teddy knew it wouldn't work for her. Her mother still found blind dates for her and she lived two hours away, plus she worked a lot of weekends.

"For about a week."

"Who were the women at the anniversary? Were they mother-finds, too?"

Adam shook his head. "During the planning process, they both stated they were bringing their own dates. Even though we were only going to be a family, we knew our mother would do something unexpected."

"Me," Teddy said.

Adam nodded. "I should have had a clue when I noticed the extra place settings, but I never thought I'd see you come through the door."

"My mother let me believe we were going to a dinner with the university organizers. The fact that it was in Smithville was a little unusual, but I wasn't expecting to join in on your parents' dinner."

Minutes later they were sitting down to a meal of omelets, sausage, toast and decaf coffee. It only took a few minutes to cook and even less to eat. Filling their cups with more coffee, Teddy added cream to hers. Adam drank his black.

"This is a better meal than the steak I had earlier tonight," Adam said.

"Last night," Teddy corrected. "It'll be daylight in three hours."

Adam took their dishes to the sink and rinsed them. Teddy got up and joined him. Together they finished the dishes and took their cups to the living room.

"Tired?" Adam asked when Teddy sank into the sofa. He joined her there.

"A little," she said, stifling a yawn. "You're going to have to go straight to the office, if you shouldn't already be there."

"I checked in before we left Smithville. I imagine the world of finance won't collapse before morning."

He put his arm around her and she leaned into him. Teddy started to giggle.

"What's so funny?" Adam asked.

"My mom, when she asked me if I could imagine being married thirty-eight years."

Adam laughed, too. "I'm sure your answer wasn't ideal for her, but you weathered it."

"I wonder what she would have thought if I'd really said what came to my mind first?"

"Which was…" Adam prompted.

"Thirty-eight years with the same man. I shudder to think." She mock shuddered and laughed, but Adam didn't join her despite his arm being around her shoulders.

"Have you ever really given it thought?" His voice

turned serious. He was holding Teddy in his arms and she couldn't see his face, but she could feel the tension that had somehow crept into his body.

Teddy moved back to look at Adam. "I never thought of being married," she answered.

"Really?" Adam's brows arched.

"Really."

"You plan weddings. Marriage ought to be the first thing on your mind."

"Or the last," she said.

"You see hundreds of couples pledging their last breath to love. You design the perfect gown and give the fantasy wedding to strangers. And not once have you ever imagined it would one day be your turn?"

Teddy hesitated a long time. "I did once," she said. "The first gown I ever designed was the one I wanted to be married in."

"The groom?"

She smiled briefly. "There was no groom. Only my fantasy of the perfect man. But I made the gown, added the finest lace. It was perfect, inside and out, and it fit every part of me."

"I bet you were a beautiful bride. I'd like to see it."

Teddy was shaking her head before Adam finished his sentence.

"Why not?" His arms tightened around her.

"I sold it."

"Why?"

"After I finished it, I took it into the office for Diana to see. She insisted I put it on. While I was dressing, a client came in. Diana was helping her when I came back. The woman saw the gown and loved it. She loved it so much tears rolled down her face. She wanted to buy it. Diana told her it wasn't for sale, but she kept asking what we'd sell it for. She was willing to pay anything. The business was new. We needed the money."

"So you sold it?"

"I sold it."

"Regrets?"

"For a while, but not anymore."

"Now you're a cynic?"

Teddy laughed. "Me? What about you?"

"Okay, we're both cynics," he agreed.

"It's a good thing we found each other."

"You know you are the most intriguing woman I've ever met?" he said.

"Really?" Teddy smiled. "Why is that?"

"I never know what you're thinking or what you're going to say."

Teddy nodded, an impish smile on her face.

"And you like that?" Adam asked.

"Absolutely."

Adam looked at her for a long time before he said, "Yeah." But he didn't stop staring at her. His eyes made Teddy warm. She saw the heat there, watched it build into desire. Her mouth went dry, and it was hard to swallow. She endured his gaze as that now-familiar blanket of warmth settled over her. She knew the heat between them would build. This time there was more. She wanted more. Anticipation, need, want. She had many names for it, but she wanted him. The slow cravings inside her spoke of arousal. Her body ached for his. She wanted his mouth on hers, his body working its primal magic with hers. She wanted to feel the weight of him, know that sweet moment of initial penetration. And she wanted to take it all the way.

Then he leaned forward. His eyes dropped to her mouth and settled there for a charged moment. Teddy licked her lips, unable to stop herself from wetting the dryness. Adam kissed her lightly, his lips brushing hers, but she felt the world tilt. She tasted the coffee from their breakfast on his mouth. It acted as an elixir, a fantastic drug with powers to transform her into the wanton tigress that was waking inside her.

The intimacy was tantalizing. Hands slipped under her hair and lifted her head to his.

Teddy's body went soft and liquid. She felt pliable, her movements like syrup, able to flow into the contours of Adam's frame as he brought her closer. Her arms, which still had substance, circled his neck, and she closed the small space separating them, connecting their mouths.

His lips changed from the soft, teasing kiss to a hard, hungry one. Adam bent her over his arm, his mouth locked on hers possessively, demanding acquiescence. Heat burned between them. Teddy gave as she got, embracing him, loving the feel of his body as her hands roamed the muscles of his back, muscles that contracted and relaxed under her sensitive fingers.

Heat built between them like the onslaught of a forest fire. Their heads bobbed one way, then the other. Teddy slid under Adam and he slid over her in a choreographed movement. His heavier frame pressed her deep into the sofa cushions. The length of him spread over her, his erection pushing against her stomach. Need sang in her veins. Adam's tongue invaded her mouth, searing her to him so tightly her breath ran out.

Teddy had never had this all-consuming experience before. She wanted to feel him all over, run her hands over his skin, feel it next to hers, have his body connect with hers and join in the ancient dance known to lovers since the beginning of time. Her dress, a thin chiffon, was a barrier to her needs.

She needed Adam, wanted him. Wanted the hot thrust of his body inside hers. Teddy always played the field. She never got close to a man. She could always control her reactions. She liked sex. She enjoyed men, but she'd never had this strong sensation of need, of anticipated release that was designed for one man. But that was what was happening with Adam. With him there was no other. Had never been another. They were forging a new frontier, terraforming a world into existence.

She wanted all of him, wanted to devour him. She wanted to get into his pants and his mind, imprint herself on him so thoroughly that her name would be visible to any other woman he ever saw.

"Have you got a condom?" Teddy asked with the small amount of breath she had.

"Yes," he said just as breathlessly.

Teddy slid off the sofa and grabbed Adam's hand. The two rushed up the steps and into her bedroom.

Adam pinned her to the door and clamped his mouth to hers the moment they were inside. For eons it seemed they stayed suspended in their own world. Then his mouth moved from hers to nibble kisses along her neck and bare shoulders. Heat mounted in the room. Teddy raised her head, giving him access to skin so sensitive she could feel the blood rising to the surface. Then Adam pulled her away from the door and reached behind her. The zipper's teeth on her dress opened with a low ripping sound as Adam pulled it down. His fingers against her back were like a match to kerosene.

Her back arched and the dress slipped to the floor. Part of the bodice contained her bra, leaving her dressed in only her panties, hosiery and high-heeled shoes. Adam opened his mouth to speak, but said nothing. He stared at her until Teddy's skin burned.

Finally, Adam slipped his arm beneath her knees and lifted her. Teddy was tall and no one had ever carried her, but Adam made her feel petite and light. He took her to the bed and laid her gently on the comforter as if she was the most precious baby. He sat next to her, one hand caressing her shoulder. It dipped down and his thumb brushed across her nipple. It sprang to life with an inner passion that was like a wave crashing against her insides.

Teddy reached up and undid the top button on his shirt. Her hands moved to the second button and released it. Adam, apparently thinking it would take too long, grabbed the back of the fabric and pulled it over his head. In the darkened light he was beautiful. His chest, bare of hair, was muscularly defined. If he carried an ounce of unneeded fat, it was well disguised.

She ran her hands over smooth skin, rising up from the bed to again join him in a kiss. This time Teddy took charge, pushing past his teeth and sweeping her tongue in his mouth. She pressed herself against him, reveling in the hardness of his chest against the softness of her breasts.

Sounds, guttural, raw and hungry, mingled about in the electrified room. Adam's hands traversed her back, angling her from side to side as their mouths danced. Suddenly, he stopped and stood, removing the remainder of his clothes, and protecting himself and her with a condom. Teddy removed her shoes, hose and panties.

Together they joined each other on the bed. She realized they both had been holding back, but now the thread that was binding their emotions snapped and they wrestled together, yearning for each other. Adam's erection pressed hard against the juncture of Teddy's legs. Sensations spiraled through her like circular lightning. She felt lit inside and out, straining for him to enter her, to make good on the promise his body invoked. With one knee he spread her legs and entered her. Teddy clamped her teeth on her lower lip but couldn't stop the sound of pleasure that escaped. Adam moved inside her, his body connected to hers, enkindling an urgency that had the two of them writhing for dominance. They rolled back and forth across the bed, their arms and legs tangling as each gave the other the joy they sought.

This was a completely new plane for Teddy. She'd never felt like this. Never had a man demanded all from her. Never was there a man she was willing to give all to before Adam. She wanted to give all. Wanted to give whatever he demanded, whatever she felt like giving.

She wanted to take it all, wanted to have him in her forever, have this feeling go on until she could no longer stand it, then have it go a little longer.

Teddy could barely breathe, but she didn't care. Her palms felt the tiny electrical impulses that ruptured off his skin as she skated her hands over the lower curve of his back. Her touch seemed to push him on. His body moved harder, faster into her. Each time his powerful body thrusted into her, the sensation of pleasure escalated. Her breath hitched as time stopped. The earth no longer moved for anyone but the two of them. Then the wave began. A huge internal signal that told her a moving ridge of passion stronger than the last was about to engulf her. She braced for it, writhing beneath him. Her body strained for the rapture, wanting it, needing it, reaching for it in every way. But it waited, a breath away, a torment so sweet that she rallied for its touch.

From a distance she heard the moan, not knowing if it came from her or Adam. Their bodies twined together, each fighting for the brass ring, identical need grasping for the golden key. Finally, Teddy heard her own voice as her climax began and ended in a scream of release.

Chapter 5

Adam rolled on his back, breathing hard. He pulled Teddy into his side and held her there, his legs entwined with hers. He didn't want to let her go. What had just happened to him? They hadn't taken the time to pull the covers down, but the bed still looked as if a war had taken place. The cover was bunched under him, although most of it had spilled to the floor. Blood throbbed in his head, yet he felt euphoric. He'd never made love like he and Teddy had just done. It was as if he was another person with her. He wanted to please her more than he ever wanted to please anyone. His own satisfaction wasn't as important to him as hers was. That had never happened before.

And he hadn't wanted to stop. He'd have gone on and on if he could, if they could. Adam ran his hand over her naked shoulder and arm. She was warm and smooth and she felt so right in his arms. The room had that electric smell of love. Adam took a deep breath, filling his lungs with their comingled scent, wishing he could capture it and save it, be able to take it out and relive this moment.

"What are you thinking?" Teddy asked. Her voice was deeper than usual, sexy in the dark, filled with satisfaction and something he couldn't define.

Adam turned to her and pushed her hair off her forehead. He kissed her lightly there, then worked his way to her lips, each kiss a thank-you for what she'd given him. Even if she was unaware of what she'd done, he thanked her.

"I was thinking that I've never felt anything like I did tonight." It was an unguarded comment. He'd never have said it in the past, but for some reason he wanted to tell her the unvarnished truth. They had been truthful with each other from the first. From the moment they met on the blind date, both had said exactly what was on their minds. Adam liked that about her.

"I felt the same way," Teddy whispered. She snugged against him. His body was cooling and he could feel the air. Teddy must be getting cold, too. Adam reached for the part of the comforter that lay on the floor and pulled it over the two of them. Like curling in a rug, they had to get closer to each other. Teddy's arm went around his waist and her body touched his from breast to his knee. Without volition he began to respond. His erection grew hard again. He wanted her again. And he wanted her now.

Pushing her back into the mattress, Adam kissed her hard. His legs covered hers and his hands trailed up and down her body, touching her skin, learning her curves, learning the zones that gave her pleasure. Because he wanted to give her pleasure. He wanted her to feel good. He wanted that more than he wanted his own gratification.

He mounted her, his body joining smoothly with hers as if they had been lovers all their lives. Adam couldn't stop the movements that seemed to come from somewhere deep inside him. Every brush of their legs together caused friction that ignited him more. He wanted to take it slower this time, but it felt like the first time. He couldn't stop the momentum that had him filling Teddy to the hilt time and again.

He heard her female sounds, listened for the pleasurable noises she made. Those sounds drove him, forced him to push harder, faster, but not over the limit. Adam waited. He needed her to join him, be with him in the frenzy of movements that would satisfy them both.

He felt it as Teddy moved. Together they convulsed, joining and separating, taking on the rhythm of their own, giving, taking, moving, writhing, learning each other. Taking the greatest pleasure on earth.

Then it happened. Adam couldn't hold back any longer. He felt Teddy climbing with him, the two of them entering that singular place that was theirs alone, the place where they burst through time and where everything was suspended. A place where their rapture had substance and the world was theirs.

Adam held her there for as long as he could. Eons

passed as his body was racked with wrenching excitement. A shocking torrent of emotion thundered through him until he thought he'd explode. Then he dropped back to earth, landing on a soft cloud. For the second time tonight, his breath came in ragged gulps. He was weak like a toddler spent from a full day of playing in the sun and sand.

And he never felt better in his life.

An insistent buzz woke Teddy. She ignored it, hoping it would stop. It came again and again. Groaning, she opened one eye. Hair obscured her view. Pushing it out of her face, she groped for her cell phone. On her first attempt, she missed, pushing the device farther away.

"Damn," she cursed. Whoever it was should call back, she thought. Glancing at the clock, it was only six o'clock. Who would be calling her this early?

Then she remembered Adam. Quickly turning over, her hand slapped the phone to the floor. The phone continued its persistence, and she expected to find Adam lying next to her. The bed was empty.

The buzz stopped.

Teddy ran a hand through her hair, sighing heavily. Disappointment flowed through her. The pillow and sheets were rumpled; he'd straightened them because their bedroom gymnastics had worked them off the bed. The night had been indescribable. But this was morning. A new day. Fantasy over. Time to return to reality.

The phone buzzed again. Teddy groaned, more at Adam being gone than the phone.

Maybe it was him, she thought and picked up the device.

"You are there," her mother said. "I thought you might have your phone off."

"Mother?" Teddy questioned, as if she didn't recognize her mother's voice.

"Of course, dear. Did I wake you?"

Teddy's mother was very active. She played tennis three mornings a week at seven o'clock. The other two mornings she swam laps in the pool at the local health club. She could swim in the university pool where she worked as an economics professor. They could also afford to have a pool in their yard, but Gemma Granville was a socializer and she met more people if she left the house than if she stayed in it.

"You were asleep. I'm sorry I woke you. I wanted to know how it went with Adam last night."

Teddy's entire blood supply bubbled to the surface, turning her red with embarrassment. She couldn't answer that question, at least not with the truth.

"What do you mean?" She stalled.

"You two were very close-headed when you left the restaurant."

"Close-headed?" Teddy didn't know what that meant.

"Close together, speaking softly, secretively, holding hands, acting like you wanted to be alone."

She was fishing for information. "We're fine, Mother. He drove me home, saw me safely into the house and…"

"And?"

Teddy heard the anticipation in her mother's voice.

"And we agreed to see each other again."

"Wonderful! I knew you two would hit it off." Gemma Granville was probably jumping up and down. "So I was right," she said.

"Right about what?"

"About Adam. He's The One."

"Mother," Teddy warned. "Don't go jumping to conclusions."

"I'm not."

"Sure you're not. You'll probably be looking at wedding gowns as soon as the stores open."

"I wouldn't look at gowns. I assume you'll design your own. After all, you *are* a designer."

Teddy rolled her eyes. "We only agreed to go on a date. Let's see how things work out?"

"But you do like him?"

Her mother was determined to get a commitment out of her. The truth was, Adam was gone. They hadn't set a date for anything else, although after last night, she was sure they would.

"Yes, Mother. I like him."

"Good."

"I have to go now, Mother. My other phone is ringing." There was no phone ringing.

"Teddy, you are coming to your dad's lecture today, right?"

"I wouldn't miss it."

"You can bring Adam."

"I'm not sure. Adam has overseas contacts and he may not be available."

"Give him a call and see. We'd love to see him again before we go back home."

"I'll see. Gotta go now." Teddy hung up, not giving her mother time to stop her.

Pushing the cover aside and untangling her legs from the bedding, she swung her legs to the floor and stood up.

She was naked.

Adam had covered her with his body and kept her warm during the night. But without the cocoon of heat the two generated, she felt the chilliness of the room.

It didn't take her long to shower and dress. Pulling on gray wool slacks and a bulky sweater, Teddy headed for the kitchen and her first cup of coffee for the day. On the counter sat a note propped against a mug with a single red rose in it. Teddy smiled. She lifted the note and read.

Sorry to leave without waking you, but you looked so adorable with your hair spread across the pillow.

It was signed, "Adam." There was a P.S. that read, "You smile in your sleep." Teddy's hand went to her hair and she pushed it through with a smile. She picked up the cup and smelled the rose. Where could Adam find a rose at this early hour or at whatever hour of the night he left?

Minutes later Teddy poured herself a cup of coffee and carried it to the table. Her phone buzzed as she sat down.

"I guess this means you're awake," Adam said.

"My mother woke me, but I got your note and your rose. Thank you."

She heard the smile in his voice. "I'd have left you a bouquet if I could have found one."

That would be romantic, Teddy thought.

"But I'm calling for a different reason."

Teddy listened, waiting for him to continue.

"My mother called this morning, too," Adam said.

"What did she want?"

"She invited us to Thanksgiving dinner."

"We knew we were going to have to be somewhere for the holiday. Although I thought that would be when our parents met. Ah, too late. We've already done that." Teddy lightened the moment she felt was getting heavy. "I guess we can split the day—do the meal with one family and dessert with the other."

"It's at least a two-hour drive to Bentonburgh and my mother had another suggestion."

Teddy set the coffee cup down and bit her bottom lip. "What is it?"

"Joint families. She'd like to invite you and your family, sisters, brothers, spouses, significant others—everyone—to Thanksgiving dinner."

"Does she know how many people she's talking about?"

"I told her you had a brother and two sisters and they may have dates. She's okay with that."

Teddy sighed.

"Are you all right?" Adam asked.

Teddy ignored his question. "I suppose she's already contacted my mother?"

"She didn't say that, but I had the feeling the deal was already done. We're the only two wild cards in the mix."

Teddy laughed. "I guess we'll be having dinner with your parents." Even though they were on the phone, Teddy thought she heard relief in his voice.

"I'll let her know."

"One more thing," she said.

"What's that?"

"My father's lecture today. My mother asked me if you would come with me. I told her you had duties at work."

"What time's the lecture?"

"Three o'clock."

"I'll pick you up at two."

"Are you sure? I mean, you—"

"Will you be ready?" he cut her off.

"Sure." This deception hadn't set well with her in the beginning. Now they were acting as if it was *real*. Combined families for Thanksgiving, joint invitations. Complications were setting in. These were minor. She couldn't imagine what was in store for them as the holidays approached.

"Teddy?" Adam said.

"I'm still here."

"I agree with you."

"About what?" she asked.

"You aren't just good in bed. You're great."

* * *

Plans were made and often they changed. Teddy knew this from her business. Working with brides, she knew that the beginning plan was not the final plan.

So when Adam called and asked if she could meet him at his condo instead of him picking her up, Teddy agreed. She wanted to see where he lived and going to his condo would give her the chance. He'd been to her house more than once, had eaten breakfast in her kitchen and spent the night in her bed. This would be her first visit to his house.

Adam lived in one of the new condo units built on the outskirts of the township. The buildings resembled town houses, but they were sold as condos. His was near the back of the complex, close to the trees that lined the property and gave the area a parklike setting.

The weather yesterday had been mild, but had turned much colder overnight. Today it was windy and bone-chilling. She thought it was ushering in November and reminding them that winter was on its way. Teddy pulled into a parking space near the front door. Shutting down the car's engine, she got out. Her booted heels clicked on the concrete. She still wore the gray slacks and sweater, but had added the pant boots, earrings and took care with her makeup.

Adam opened the door as soon as she rang the bell. He smiled when he saw her, and took her hand to draw her inside.

"Oops," she said, facing him. "I forgot to get you a gift."

"Gift?"

"My mother says the first time you go to visit someone, you should bring them a gift. I don't have one." She spread her hands, showing their emptiness.

"I'll take this instead."

He leaned forward and kissed her. It was short and only intended to be a friendly kiss. But when he pulled away, the two looked at each other and in the next moment, she was in his arms for a full never-let-me-go liplock. It went on for several seconds, before he raised his head.

"That will take the chill off the weather outside," Teddy said to cover the fact that if they didn't have to go to her father's lecture, she'd push him to the floor and make love to him right here. She needed to control herself around him. This was a deception for their parents, but she was having trouble separating fact from fiction.

Adam laughed. "I'm almost ready. Make yourself comfortable. I'll be right back."

"Isn't that a woman's line?"

"It's interchangeable. You can use it next time I come to pick you up."

He disappeared up the stairs and Teddy turned around. The prickles on her arms were receding. Removing her coat, she laid it on a chair inside the living room. There was a fireplace and a fire burned in the hearth. Teddy spread her hands, taking in the warmth while she looked about. The room had that decorated-by-a-decorator look. Everything coordinated: the walls were a soft blue-gray, blond hardwood floors that glowed warm in almost any light. The furniture was black leather, soft as butter with gray and white pillows. Fresh flowers were set strategically about the room, giving unexpected pops of color and a fragrance that had her thinking of romance. Spying a vase of roses, she went to it, bending down and smelling their fragrance. Now she knew where he got the rose he'd left her. He'd driven all the way home and come back to leave her a rose. Emotion welled up in her throat and she had to blink away the tears that filled her eyes. The simple act of kindness was unexpected.

There were pictures on the walls, not anything personal. These were oil paintings. Teddy didn't know art, but she knew these weren't the kind of paintings you find in local department stores. Looking in the corner of one, she checked for a signature. It was hard to read and meant nothing to her. Despite the room's perfection, it was cold. There was nothing here that said Adam. None of the personality she was coming to know was reflected in the blacks and grays of the room.

He was a warm man, sensitive and loving. Of course, his humor could use some work, but that was one of the things that made him different from all other men.

"Ready?" Adam asked, running down the stairs.

Teddy faced him. Wearing pants that hugged his thighs and a blue shirt open at the collar, he looked both casual and good enough to eat. Teddy curled her fingers in her hands to keep them from reaching out and touching him. She knew that body, knew the hardness of his chest, the strength of the muscles in his arms and the tenderness they could enfold. She knew his mouth, the way it fit perfectly over hers. The way his tongue felt sweeping into her mouth and removing everything from her mind except him.

"You brought me a rose," she said, placing her hand on one of the buds in the vase.

"Sleeping so soundly, you reminded me of a delicate flower."

"So you drove home, picked a flower and drove back."

"It was on the way to work."

She knew he was making light of his actions, but she appreciated it. Teddy went to him and kissed him on the cheek. "I liked the rose."

"You're easy to satisfy."

"Am I?" she questioned, knowing the innuendo in her voice.

Adam darkened, but recovered almost immediately. "I'm not sure. I'll have to try it again just to make sure."

She kissed him again, this time on the mouth. "Now?"

He let out a long breath. "I would sure like to, but we'll miss your father's lecture and your mother will never let us live it down."

"True." She pouted.

"We'd better go before I change my mind. And if we don't leave now, we're bound to get caught in traffic."

"Right," Teddy said.

"Would you hand me the phone in that drawer?" He indicated an end table. Teddy hadn't seen the drawer when she looked around the room. She heard Adam exhale a long breath when she was no longer looking at him. The thought that she affected him made her feel good.

Pulling the drawer open, she saw a phone lying in the bottom. The only other thing in the drawer was a charger the phone was connected to. She didn't see how it fed out the back or bottom of the drawer and connected to an outlet. Reaching inside she disconnected the phone. The password screen came up as she handed it to him.

Adam slipped it into the pocket of the leather jacket he'd added to his wardrobe.

Lifting Teddy's coat from the chair, he held it as she slipped her arms inside. For a brief moment he squeezed her shoulders. She wanted to step back into his embrace, feel the warmth of him, but she knew where that would lead. Where she wanted it to lead. But they didn't have time for that now.

"We've been invited to a Christmas party," Adam said.

"Really?"

"One of my VPs holds a holiday party every year. Since we'll still be together then, would you like to go?"

"I haven't been to a party just for pleasure in a long time," she said. "I'd love to."

"Good. I'll let him know we're coming."

"Now, we'd better get to this party."

With his hand on the small of her back, the two went through the front door. Teddy opened her car door and slipped inside. The decision of who would drive had been solved without discussion.

As an honored guest, Teddy had a pass to park on campus. They entered the lecture hall several minutes later and took seats near the middle of the auditorium.

"What's your father speaking about?" Adam asked. "I know it has something to do with journalism, but I didn't get the specific topic."

"I'm fuzzy on that," Teddy said. "He told me, but I wasn't paying close attention. My mother was trying to get into the discussion and I was blocking her. It has something to do with the future in the digital arena of journalism."

Teddy turned her attention to the program, looking for the topic. She didn't get to read it due to the interruption.

"There you two are," her mother said, coming to where they sat. Her voice sounded like a proud parent on the night of her daughter's first date. "I thought you'd like to sit closer to the front."

Teddy shook her head. "If we sit up there, Father will embarrass me. This is fine." They were sitting in the subdued light halfway up the hall. Teddy wasn't sure they could be seen from the front.

The room got quiet. "They're about to start," her mother whispered. "I'll see you when the lecture is over." She got up and rushed back to her seat near the front, hunching down as if she didn't want to be seen.

When the president of the symposium introduced her father, he said the speech was on the coexistence of the internet and the small newspaper. Adam took her hand as her father walked to the podium and began his speech. Neither she nor Adam had anything to do with newspapers. The subject sounded boring, but her father had a knack for entertainment and he had the audience laughing as he delivered anecdotes on his experiences as a newsman from the big papers to the one he managed now. His lecture was followed by an active question and answer period.

The crowd thinned until only Adam, Teddy and her mother remained in the audience. Several organizers of the event cornered her father and congratulated him.

"Are you going back to work after this?" Teddy asked Adam.

"I thought we might have an early dinner with your parents."

"You're ready to endure my mother again so soon?" Teddy's eyebrows went up while her voice went down.

"I can take it." He smiled, glancing at the woman sitting in the first row.

"They're not staying," Teddy told him. "They decided to return home right away. My father can't be away from his paper too long. He gets withdrawal symptoms."

"So, it's just you and me?"

"If you can endure me so soon after the last time," she teased.

Adam's eyes turned dark and hot. She meant to be flippant, get a laugh out of him, but the impact of her words after the night they'd spent together came to her in a rush of heat. By the look on Adam's face, he was obviously remembering that night, too.

"Teddy?"

She didn't even hear her mother until she'd called

her name twice. Turning, she looked at her, hoping it was too dim in the room for her mom to see her clearly.

"We're going to head for home as soon as your father finishes up." She glanced at the three men still talking at the front of the room.

"We want to get there before dark," her father was saying.

It was only a couple of hours to Bentonburgh. They should make it with time to spare. But it was rush hour and that would slow them down a bit.

Teddy and Adam stood up and went to the end of the aisle. Adam followed. Teddy hugged her mother. And then her mom hugged Adam. It appeared as if she was welcoming him to the family.

"Adam, it was good seeing you again. And I spoke with Ann this morning. We agreed to spend Thanksgiving as a family."

"Mom," Teddy warned again.

"What?" She looked at Teddy. "It'll be good to spend the day with friends and family."

"Thanksgiving is a month away."

"But these things must be planned, the same as weddings."

"Mrs. Granville, I'm looking forward to it," Adam cajoled, slipping his arm around Teddy's waist. She let go of her rising anger.

Her mom stepped back. "You two do make a lovely couple. And I can see how much you love each other."

Teddy grabbed Adam's hand and squeezed. Neither of them agreed or disagreed with Gemma Granville's comment.

Finally her father joined the group. The four of them left the auditorium and walked to his SUV.

"I wish we could stay longer, but I have to get back to the paper," Merle Sullivan said. He reached around her to Adam and shook his hand. The two men nodded mutually. Both knew it wasn't necessary. Then her dad kissed her on the forehead and climbed into the driver's seat. Her mom got in the passenger seat and fastened her seat belt. With a honk of the horn, they pulled out of the parking lot and headed south toward Maryland. Teddy stood with Adam's arm around her until the SUV was out of sight.

"What do you think they're planning for Thanksgiving?" Teddy asked.

"I have no idea. But I realize this was just a warm-up. The main event is being planned as we speak."

"I can only hope we'll be ready for it," Teddy said.

"We'll surprise them."

Chapter 6

Both Teddy and Diana were early risers. This was something that made them compatible. They had time to spend a few minutes being friends and then get a jump on the day. The calm before the storm, before the other associates came in and before the phones started to ring.

"You're here early," Diana said. "You're always early, but today you're really early."

"After spending two days with my parents and the weekend, I have a thousand things to do. Why are you here at—" she looked at her watch "—six o'clock?"

"Scott had an early flight. I dropped him at the airfield."

Scott usually drove himself to the airport, but he and Diana were still technically newlyweds. She made no excuses about wanting to be with him as much as possible. And Scott had told her he loved finding her at the airport waiting for him when he returned from his flights.

Diana took a seat and handed Teddy the cup of coffee she often brought in with her. "When I spoke with Renee on Friday, she seemed to have everything under control."

"She did. I told you she's ready to go out on her own. I'm going to hate losing her as an assistant."

"I'm sure you two will work something out." Diana leaned forward, putting her arm on the edge of the desk. "Tell me about your weekend. Did you have a good time?"

Teddy leaned back. "Picture this—two mothers, both wanting their children to find someone and get married. Send them all out to dinner and miraculously discover they are all at the same restaurant and in the same room."

Diana was holding her mouth closed. "You met Adam's parents."

"And his two brothers and their dates."

Diana was laughing. "What an ambush."

"That's exactly the word Adam used."

Teddy explained that her mother led her to believe they were going to dinner as guests of the university, but it was really to join the Sullivans for their anniversary, and for them to push Adam and her toward each other.

"Stop laughing," Teddy said, trying to keep from joining her. "It's not funny."

"It's hilarious, and to think they aren't even trying to hide their strategy." She took a drink of her coffee. "How's Adam taking it?"

The mention of his name had Teddy's body reacting as if she could touch him from this distance. She hoped Diana didn't notice the change.

"He's better than I expected he'd be. This was his idea, but I thought he hadn't thought it through. Yet, he falls into the act as if it was natural."

Teddy looked up and saw Diana staring at her. "Are you falling for him?" The scrutiny in her eyes was serious.

"Of course not." She wanted to stop there but knew she needed to reinforce her statement. "He is easy to look at."

"And he's got a great body."

Teddy nearly choked.

"And he loves to touch you," Diana went on.

"What?"

"Don't tell me you haven't noticed."

"He's only doing that for show," Teddy explained.

"Yeah," Diana said. "It isn't only that he touches you, but the way he touches you."

"The way?" Teddy frowned.

Teddy knew exactly what Diana meant. She loved being touched by Adam. Whenever he put his hands on her, she felt his tenderness. She wanted to turn into his arms and settle there forever.

"Teddy, you're blushing."

Teddy snapped out of the reverie she was falling into. "I am not."

Diana didn't respond. At least, not in words. She gazed at Teddy for a long time.

"All right, I'm attracted to him. And yes, I've noticed that he touches me a lot."

"And you like it." It was a statement.

"I shouldn't. I shouldn't feel anything more than a warm hand, but for some reason my entire body almost glows."

"I am so glad to hear this."

"Why?" Teddy asked.

"Because you deserve to be happy."

"You're only saying that because you found Scott and you think everyone should feel like you do."

"You're right," Diana said. "What I feel for Scott is amazing. And I never thought he'd be the man for me, but since that time long ago, you've sort of given up on ever finding someone. But with Adam—"

"Stop." Teddy put her hand up. "There is no Adam and me. We're not a couple. We're only together for this short period. He and I set the rules and we'll live by them."

"Teddy, things always change. You know that."

"Not this," Diana said.

"Does he feel the same way about you?"

"I don't know," Teddy said, sorry this conversation had taken this turn.

"Does he know how you feel?"

Teddy shook her head. She hoped he didn't know.

The jewelry store on the corner of Nassau and Williams Street had sat there for decades. Adam passed it almost daily, but he'd never stopped to look into the windows. Yet today he stood there, staring at a setting in the window. *Would Teddy like that?* he wondered. He pictured the ring decorating her elegant hand.

"Never buy the ring unless she's there to pick it out," someone said behind him. Adam turned to find Veronica Woods standing behind him. She was the last person he ever expected to find on a street in Princeton.

"Veronica, this is a surprise."

"A good one, I hope," she said. She leaned forward to kiss him. Adam pushed his cheek to hers and stepped back. Veronica was dressed impeccably in black and white, looking like someone he'd see on the cover of a glossy magazine. Her long coat was ringed with white fur around the neck and sleeves. On her head sat a matching hat. This framed her face, softened her features and made her desirable to any man—except him.

"What are you doing here? I thought you moved out to Chicago."

"I did. I'm only back for a visit, but I'll be here for a couple of weeks. When I left, I took a job working for a decorator. After a few years, I joined the partnership. A while after that, I was about to strike out on my own when we decided to open another office. I'm running that office."

"Here in Princeton?" Veronica represented betrayal to him and he didn't want to be reminded of it constantly. He knew she'd never really been in love with him, but the humiliation she heaped on him was not easily forgotten.

"Philadelphia," she corrected with a shake of her

head. "I came up today to see some old friends. I didn't know one of them would be you. I take it you're still running that investment company."

He nodded, disappointed that she didn't remember the name of his company. He could tell Veronica hadn't changed much. She looked better than she had five years ago. Her clothes were designer originals, but her values were the same. She acted as if they'd parted as friends, as if nothing had occurred between them.

"Things must be going well if you're looking in the window of a jewelry store." She indicated the display windows behind him. "Who is she?"

Adam glanced at the window. The setting he'd been looking at sparkled. "You wouldn't know her," he replied. Adam hadn't seen anyone on a steady basis since he and Veronica's relationship had ended. He wasn't about to let her think he was harboring any residual feelings for her.

"It must be serious. I never thought you'd give up your bachelorhood."

"Change happens," he said, refusing to mention anything about their past.

She smiled. Adam knew that look, knew that the sweeping down of her eyelashes meant she was covering something she didn't want him to see.

"Why don't you buy me a cup of coffee and tell me about her?"

He looked over her shoulder at the university that dominated the college town. "I'd love to, but I have to get back to that investment company. I only stepped out to pick up my lunch, which is probably ready by now. But it was great seeing you again." He knew he was dismissing her. "Good luck with your design firm."

She opened her purse and pulled out a business card. "Call me sometime."

He took the card. "If I need a decorator."

"Or if you just want to mull over good times."

Adam doubted he would call for that reason, but he nodded. Veronica again leaned forward. This time she kissed his mouth. And of course it would happen then. As he raised his head he saw two women turn the corner and walk toward them. Immediately he recognized them both.

Teddy and Diana.

It took a moment since they were talking to each other before Teddy recognized him and smiled. The two approached.

"Hello, Adam," Teddy said. She glanced at the woman and nodded.

"Veronica, this is Theresa Granville, my fiancée, and her business partner, Diana Thomas."

As the women acknowledged each other, Teddy reached into her purse and extracted a tissue. She held it out to Adam.

Red wasn't his color.

At seven o'clock that night Teddy stood outside Adam's condo. She pushed the doorbell and heard it chiming through the ornate entryway.

"So that was Veronica?" Teddy stated by way of a greeting as Adam opened the door.

"That was Veronica." Adam sighed. He stood back

and allowed her to enter the foyer. Taking her coat, he hung it in the hall closet. "I assume you're hungry and since I didn't know what you might want to eat, I bought a variety of entrées."

He led her into the dining room, where several bowls of Chinese food sat on a table set for two. She'd glanced in the kitchen on the way and saw the paper containers whose contents he'd transferred to china bowls. She wondered what Adam was trying to do, what he might want to tell her.

"Sit down," he said and poured her a glass of white wine.

Teddy took a seat and because she was hungry, she filled her plate with a small sample of everything and ate heartily. Adam, on the other hand, pushed his food around but ate very little. He felt guilty, she thought.

"Adam, is something wrong?"

"Why do you ask that?"

She was sure something more was wrong than she thought. In her experience, any time a question was answered with a question meant something was wrong. Their meeting on the street this afternoon had prompted her to rethink their plan.

"What is it?" she asked.

Adam got up and took his wineglass. He offered his hand to Teddy and they moved from the dining table to the large family room. This one also looked as if a decorator had a hand in the furnishings and wall art. It had a large circular sofa facing a gigantic television and a fireplace with a fire that crackled and popped, adding ambiance to the evening meal. Teddy took a seat on the sofa.

She finally spoke. "Is this about Veronica?"

Teddy felt the tension rising in her. She didn't know how this was going to end, but she didn't think it would come out in her favor. Adam turned to her and Teddy knew the look. It was an ending. Everything had been packed and was ready for release. Teddy just needed to wait for the last train.

"Is she your one and only? I know the rules we set in place when we started this. But if you want to end the pretense so you can be with—"

Teddy didn't get any further. Adam moved faster than lightning. He was in front of her, pulling her up from her seat. His face was so close to hers it scared her. "This is not about Veronica. I saw your face this afternoon. You looked as if I'd kicked you."

Teddy pulled back, taking a step to straighten herself. "Things are getting complicated," she said. "More so than we thought they would. Now you have a former lover in town."

"Emphasis on 'former.' Our relationship ended long ago. It's old news."

"Is it?" she asked.

"Very old," he confirmed.

"It didn't look old. In fact, it looked as if there would be a new edition. And I thought in light of that, you might want to end this. Now." He was holding her so close and so tight, she could hardly breathe. "I thought you and Veronica wanted to get together. After all, you *were* wearing her lipstick."

Adam's head moved with the same speed as he'd crossed the room. His mouth clamped on hers and held for a long moment, long enough for Teddy to cling to him. These days that took less than a second.

"Now I'm wearing yours," he said.

Teddy couldn't stop the smile that turned her mouth up. The smile became a giggle and then a laugh. Adam put his arms around her and together they laughed. The tension that had settled between them on the main street in Princeton that afternoon lifted.

Adam took her hands and they sat side by side on the sofa. The fire gave the room a rosy glow. Teddy slipped her feet out of her shoes and tucked them under her.

Adam smiled. "Comfortable?"

She nodded. "Tell me about her?"

"I told you the story before."

"And there's nothing more?"

"Nothing."

"But she's back now. More than likely you'll run into her from time to time."

"She's a decorator. She's opening a business in Philly. Probably more of her clients will be in that area than here."

Teddy felt he was giving her excuses, rationalizations that could boil over and change at any given moment.

"Was she The One, Adam? Did you think the two of you would have the forever kind of love?"

He hesitated a long time. He took a drink of his wine but didn't move away from Teddy. She felt for a change in his body, a stiffening of muscles that indicated an increased heartbeat or a rush of blood to the head, even a raised eyebrow. None of the cues were present.

"My brother Quinn says there comes a time when you have to risk your heart. I thought I was doing that with Veronica. I thought she felt the same about me. That proved not to be the case."

"So you're no longer willing to risk your heart?" Teddy asked. "I guess that makes me perfect for you."

His head snapped up. "How so?"

"Your plan. The Marriage Pact. It's perfect. There's no chance of you risking anything. You can satisfy your inner logic of never letting a woman entangle you the way Veronica did without the burden of complications."

"That's not what this is about," he protested.

"Are you sure?" Teddy raised her eyebrows, giving him an inquiring look. Her heart was beating so fast, she didn't know if she could speak, but she understood everything now. She knew there was more to this deception than just eluding his mother's attempts to have him find a bride. He'd built a wall around his heart and Teddy was the temporary guard who would keep the wall intact for a while. Then he'd move on to the next guard or retreat into his overseas connections as a method of keeping himself free of risks.

"What do you think this is about?" he asked.

"That's a loaded question. Are you sure you want the answer?"

His face wasn't exactly blank, but Teddy could see he was trying to keep it free of expression. He nodded. "I'm a big boy. I can take it."

Teddy uncurled her feet and stood up. Taking her

wineglass, she walked about the room. "A decorator did this room, didn't she?"

Adam frowned. She knew he didn't understand the question.

"Veronica has never been here," he said.

"I didn't think it was her," Teddy told him. "It's a beautiful room. I could see it in one of the glossy magazines."

"But," he prompted.

She came back to him. Faced him. She sat on the huge coffee table that held only a glass vase of flowers, her knees only an inch from his.

"There's nothing of you in this room. There's nothing of you in the entire house. Not even in the bedroom." She paused, giving him a long look. "Maybe the flowers are your reflection, which are surprising since most men would never think of flowers, especially fresh ones. Few would buy them or replace them when they died."

"Or drive home to get a single red rose?"

Teddy smiled remembering the mug on her kitchen table the first time they made love. The thought nearly undid her. That warm blanket began to settle, but she pushed it aside. She needed to stay on track. Allowing thoughts of their lovemaking would send her soaring in a different, although wonderful, direction.

"That, too," she said. "Only the flowers say you have a heart, much less want to risk it." She took his hand. He didn't pull it away, but it had gone from warm to slightly cold. "I'm sorry your don't like what I'm saying, but you did ask. I hope you see that, like your brother said, without risk there is no love, and without love, you'll have a very lonely existence."

Adam pulled her up from the table and onto his lap. "So you believe I should let go of the past and open my heart?"

Her own heart was beating a drum in his ears. She nodded.

"Are you also saying I should approach Veronica and see if what I thought we had in the past could be rekindled? Bring the fire back to life?"

Teddy forcibly controlled her urge to move out of his arms. "If that is what you want," she whispered.

"That's not what I want."

She raised her eyelids and stared directly at him. She knew she shouldn't ask, but she had to know. "What do you want?"

"Right now? Right this very moment?"

"Yes," she said, drawing the word out as if it had several syllables.

"I want you."

"I want you" wasn't the same as "I love you." Adam knew that. He wanted to say it, wanted to let Teddy know that she meant more to him than any woman ever had, but he couldn't get the words out. So he retreated, retreated into what any man would do in his situation.

He kissed her.

Teddy didn't protest. She was pliant in his arms. He wanted her there, wanted to tell her everything she wanted to know, but he'd been burned before.

* * *

It was hard to think there was hunger in the world when Teddy looked at all the food on the tables in Dr. Sullivan's dining room. She said "tables," since there were at least three. They were covered with turkey, salads, sweet potatoes, green bean casseroles, corn bread dressing, pies, cakes and even more dishes, all smelling delicious and making her stomach growl.

Just as both mothers were trying to get their offsprings married, both mothers were outdoing the other with the amount of food they cooked and delivered. Her sisters Sienna and Sierra brought their signature dishes. Emory, her brother, was exempt since he'd proven years ago that cooking wasn't something he would excel at. Teddy arrived with a dish of macaroni and cheese.

"Who do you think will win?" Galen whispered in Adam's ear.

Adam glanced at the football game on the big-screen television, but he knew his brother wasn't speaking of the game.

"You don't even want to go there," Adam said. "It could get bloody."

"Just remember," Quinn joined in. "Everything is delicious. Nothing is better than the other."

"They are all equally great," Adam and Galen said in unison.

"Obviously you three have gone through this routine before," Teddy said.

Quinn nodded. "And we learned early not to play favorites."

"Remember that time everyone made the green

beans and wanted all the cousins to judge them?" Quinn asked, laughter in his question.

Galen frowned. "That year I was sure someone would die."

They were all laughing at a shared memory. Teddy knew from her own family that the rivalry was all in good fun. She hadn't made a green bean casserole. Her dish was macaroni and cheese, which sat on a warming plate in the dining room. Teddy was free to join the others and enjoy the game. Dr. Sullivan had already refused any additional help in the kitchen.

"So," Galen said, looking at Adam, "when are you two getting married?"

The room went quiet. Everyone stared at Galen.

"What?" Galen asked, spreading his arms in innocence, one of them holding a beer. "You've been going out for months. This is the second family dinner you've appeared at." He glanced at Teddy. "It must be time for marriage."

"We'll set ours when you set yours," Teddy told him.

"Me?"

"Yes, I have a sister and I see how you look at her." Teddy checked that her sister Sienna couldn't hear her. "I'll point that out to your mother. Then all we'll need is one more dinner and it can be a double wedding."

Again, the room stared at the youngest Sullivan son.

Finally Quinn laughed and, pointing at his brother, said, "She got you." Everyone burst into laughter.

Obviously embarrassed, Galen was the first to stand up when his mom announced the meal. The dining room didn't have the same dimensions as the restaurant where their anniversary dinner was held. Instead of a U-shaped arrangement, two parallel tables had been set up. Adam steered her to one the farthest from both their parents.

For the next twenty minutes, food was passed around, plates were filled, and the only sounds in the room were those of the dinner forks and "Mmm, mmm" of appreciation.

"Overwhelmed yet?" Adam asked.

"I'm actually enjoying myself," Teddy told him. And she was. "How about you?"

"I love my family. We don't get together often enough."

"I know. Despite our parents' meddling, we have so much to be thankful for."

Adam gave her one of those looks, the one that said so much but told her so little. It was confusing, making her wonder what he was thinking. What was behind the look? And what did it mean?

"My brothers really like you." He took a moment to glance around the table. Teddy followed his gaze. Everyone was eating and talking, smiling, making comments on how good the food was. Galen sat next to Teddy's sister Sienna, and the two seemed to be hitting it off.

"You have a nice family," Teddy said.

"Even my mother?"

"Especially your mother. She's only looking out for your best interest."

Adam's eyes opened wide. "Who are you and where have you hidden Theresa Granville?"

She laughed. "Every parent wants their children to be happy."

"And they want grandchildren."

"That, too," Teddy agreed.

"But most of them don't size up dates for them," Adam said, keeping his voice low enough that no one else could hear him.

Before Teddy could answer, Dr. Sullivan announced dessert. The groan of being too full to take another bite came up like the roar of a football goal.

"I'll have some later," Quinn said.

"Then I guess we can fill our glasses with wine. And you guys can clean up the plates," his mom said.

En masse, the women left the room and by mutual agreement, the guys cleared away the dishes. By the time they finished and joined the group in the great room, the first game was almost over.

"Wine?" Adam asked, coming to stand by Teddy. Teddy nodded, handing him her glass. Instead of him leaving, he squatted down beside her. "Anything happen while I was gone?"

She shook her head. "Everyone was really into the game. I see your mom is a big fan."

"She is now." He glanced at her. "My father recruited her, and when she was the only woman in a house of men, it was conform or be left out."

Teddy watched him smile. He really loved his family. She liked that about him. When they'd first met, she'd classified him as a loner, someone you assumed sprang full grown without the aid of parents. But in the past weeks, Teddy had come to know the man inside and she was falling further and further in love with him.

"What's that look for?" Adam asked.

"What look?"

"The one on your face. It's an I've-got-a-secret face. Like you know something no one else does."

"I might," she answered honestly, but couched it behind an impish grin to throw him off. Then she leaned over and kissed him quickly. "That's my secret."

"Not anymore," Adam said. "My mother saw that."

"Good," Teddy whispered. "Let's give her a show." Her mouth was only a shadow away from his. "Just a short comedy, not a Broadway musical." She kissed him again, a slow sweet touching of lips. Adam slid his tongue between the seam of her lips. Lightning strikes thundered through her blood. She moved back before a production number started and she was unable to stop.

"I'll get that wine now."

Chapter 7

The last bottle of wine on the table was empty. Adam took it to the kitchen and dropped it in the recycle bin. Getting a new bottle, he pulled the cork out. Ann Sullivan entered the kitchen as it popped. She took a seat on one of the high stools in front of the large center counter. The food from dinner sat in myriad plastic containers stacked at the end closest to the refrigerator.

"Did I hear you talking about setting a date earlier? Was that a wedding date?"

His mom didn't begin with small talk. She went right to the subject on her mind.

"Mom, don't go jumping over the horse." Adam poured wine in the two glasses. Teddy's glass had her lip print arched on the delicate crystal. He had the urge to drink from that glass, placing his mouth on the exact spot where hers had been.

"I'm not, but my hearing is excellent."

"It was a joke. Galen was teasing Teddy. Did you hear her reply?"

Ignoring his question, she said, "All teasing aside, the two of you have been seeing a lot of each other. And from what I saw in there, you both seem to only have eyes for each other. Is this arrangement exclusive?"

"We've never discussed that specifically, but I'm not seeing anyone else at the moment. I'm sure Teddy isn't, either."

His mom smiled, obviously pleased. Then her face became serious again. "You'll never guess who I saw yesterday while I was running some last-minute errands."

Adam moved to the seat next to his mother. He slipped into the chair and looked directly at her. "Let me guess. Veronica Woods."

She raised her brows in surprise. "You know she's back?"

"She's not back. She says she's here to do a job based in Philly. She was only here visiting."

"Where did you two meet?"

"I ran into her outside of Varrick's and before you ask, there is nothing left between us. We've been done for some time now."

"Varrick's? Varrick's Jewelry?"

"One and the same," Adam said. "But I'm sure you already know this. Veronica isn't one to keep information to herself if she can use it."

"You were looking at rings." It was a statement.

"I was out for lunch and looked in the windows. I wasn't shopping."

"So you didn't buy Teddy a ring?" Adam's mother's voice went slightly up at the end of the sentence in hope that he'd tell her he had bought a ring.

"Isn't it true that the woman should always be there to pick out her own ring?"

She nodded. "Are you in the market for a ring?"

"Do you think it's too soon? We've only known each other a few months."

She shook her head. "I don't think it's too soon." Ann Sullivan slid down from her chair and folded Adam in her outstretched arms.

After a second, Adam pushed her back "You're not just saying that because you want grandchildren, are you?"

"Of course not." She feigned hurt. "You know I want grandchildren, but I also want you to be happy. You *are* in love with Teddy, right?"

There it was, Adam thought. He'd walked right into that question. And it had to be answered. If he were a lawyer, he would never set himself up for a question he didn't want to answer. But Adam wasn't a lawyer. And he'd drawn the question.

"Yes," he said. The word came lowly as if he was talking to himself. He did love Teddy. He only realized it this minute. When had that happened?

"Are you going to ask her to marry you?"

Adam was having difficulty processing this newly discovered information, but his mom's question penetrated his brain. "Mom, slow down. Let me do this in my way. Teddy may not feel that we've known each other long enough. She may not feel the same way about me."

"From what I saw a few minutes ago, her love is something you should have no doubt of."

"In any case, I'll tell her when the time is right," Adam said.

"Of course. You know I would never interfere."

Adam picked up the two wineglasses and howled.

A loud shout punched the air in the family room as the supported NFL team scored a touchdown. Hands slapped in the air. Calls of success, as if they were the actual player, filled the airspace from floor to ceiling. It appeared the Sullivans and the Granvilles had bonded. Teddy's brother and sisters were in the mix of Adam's family, comfortable and easy as if they had been friends for years.

Teddy looked over her shoulder for any sign of Adam. He came out of the kitchen first. His mother followed. Teddy watched, hoping to find something in his expression that would tell her what his mom thought of their demonstration before he left to get her wine. Adam's face was unreadable, but his mom had a smile on hers and a gleam in her eyes.

Teddy got up and met him near the dining room door. "What happened in there?" she asked as soon as his mother passed out of earshot. He set the wineglasses on the table and the two took seats. She had her back to the room. Taking a sip of the wine, she felt she might need fortification.

"She wanted to know about Veronica."

"What about her?"

"She asked if I still had any feelings for her."

"And…" Teddy wanted to know the answer to that, too.

"You're not jealous, are you?" He smiled at her and took her hand.

Teddy understood he was teasing, and she *was* jealous. But she couldn't tell him that. "Of course I'm not jealous." She paused, both hands cradling her glass. "We already discussed this and resolved it. I don't think your mother was really interested in Veronica," Teddy said.

"You weren't even in there. How could you know?" Adam asked.

"She was probing you for information about us." The look on his face told her she'd hit the mark. "What did you tell her?"

"That I was in love with you and planning to ask you to marry me."

Teddy laughed. "Sure you did."

"You don't believe me?"

"If you'd told her that, she'd have come out of that kitchen singing your praises." She stopped him from responding by going on. "I know because it's what my mother would do."

Behind her, Teddy heard a commotion. Her mother was making a beeline for her. Teddy stiffened, understanding that something was about to happen. Teddy glanced at Adam. "You didn't," she said.

"Teddy, is it true? Why didn't you tell me?" her mother said. She was excited, her color heightened and a smile on her face like George Bailey's when he realized it really was a wonderful life. "I should have been the first to know."

"What?" Teddy asked. She felt Adam's hand tighten on hers. She looked at him, but his eyes were piercing his mother's as if she had also betrayed him.

Teddy's mother looked at Adam. "I believe Adam has something to ask you."

Teddy swung her gaze from Adam to her mother. She saw his face fall.

"Mom, I asked you—"

"I'm sorry, Adam. I didn't think Gemma would rush over and spill the beans."

"I don't understand," Teddy said, but apprehension gripped her.

"Go on, Adam," his mom prompted. "The cat's out of the bag now."

Teddy looked at the room. The television commentator continued his play-by-play. The field of bulked up men scrambled and ran for a goal line, but no one in the household watched them. All eyes were trained on her and Adam.

Adam curled his hand in hers. "This isn't how I pictured it," he told her. "I thought we'd have a romantic evening and then I'd ask you."

"Ask me?" There was a warning underlying Teddy's

question. He couldn't be about to do what she thought he would do. This was not part of the plan.

"Will you marry me?"

Collectively, the room held its breath. Teddy held hers, too. Her hands went ice-cold. Adam felt it, but he didn't take his gaze away from her. She had to answer. She couldn't wait too long or her mother would begin to worry or she'd answer for her.

Teddy looked at him. An unexpected film of mist blurred her eyes. "Yes," she said.

The breaths were exhaled.

Adam got up and pulled her into his arms. He kissed her. And then hugged her to him.

"You are so going to pay for this," Teddy whispered into his neck.

Adam held on to Teddy. He didn't want to push her back. However, this time it wasn't because he loved holding her. He didn't want to see the look in her eyes. She had tears in them and while the others would interpret them as those of a blushing bride, Adam knew they weren't happy tears. He'd just been forced into a corner, behind a web of lies that was tightening with every day and every step they took.

Pandemonium broke out. Teddy was pulled away from Adam and hugged by her mother, then her brother and sisters in turn. Adam's mother and his family followed. Everyone was congratulating them.

The wine was exchanged for champagne, and toasts to the happy couple were shared. Adam kept track of

Teddy. He wanted to get to her and explain, but something or someone stopped him.

"This is great, Adam," Quinn said. "Now Galen and I will be released from the pressure chamber." He laughed and slapped his brother on the back. "Seriously, though, I like Teddy. I'm sure the two of you will be happy."

"When are you going to get the ring?" Adam's mother asked.

"I have an idea." Teddy's mom cut in. "I have to return that painting to the gallery in New York. Why don't we go up there next week? I can return the painting and get the right one. You two can go pick out a ring and we can all have lunch at The Gaslight."

"No," Teddy said. Her voice was a little more emphatic than Adam knew she'd expected it to be.

The two mothers stared at her.

"I'm sorry," she apologized. "This has been a little overwhelming. Adam and I need a little time to discuss things." She reached for Adam's hand and he immediately took it and pulled her into his side.

"Of course," her mother said. She came forward and hugged Teddy again. "We can talk about this later."

Gemma Granville turned back to Adam's mom. With all the excitement of a bride herself, she said, "Ann, we're going to have a wedding in the family." The two women hugged and jumped up and down like children.

Adam closed his eyes and wondered how this had gotten so out of control.

* * *

Snow! The white puffy flakes should have surprised Teddy when they left Adam's parents' house and headed back to Princeton, but she was in no mood to care about the weather. Her life was falling apart. Both families were still celebrating, hugging them, waving goodbye, wishing them well as if they had already married and were off for their honeymoon.

Teddy's parents and three siblings were staying with her. She knew they had taken a turn about the house looking for evidence that she and Adam were living together or at least leaving clothing and various grooming items around.

While Adam had spent the night several times, he'd left nothing behind, no toothbrush in the bathroom, no forgotten clothing in the closet or drawers. If he had, Teddy would have found and returned them before her family descended. She'd given the place a good cleaning. Although neither her mother nor any of her siblings were white-glove people, Teddy always cleaned like a mad woman when they were planning to stay over. Now she wouldn't be going back there tonight. She and Adam had a lot to talk about, if she could even begin to talk.

"What were you thinking?" Teddy attacked him the moment they were in the car. "This was not part of the plan. We never talked about getting engaged, never discussed an engagement. This…this sham is supposed to be over by Christmas. Now what are we going to do?"

Adam glanced at her and sighed heavily, but he said nothing. In fact, the two of them remained quiet for the duration of the twenty-minute ride. When he made the turn that led to her house, Teddy spoke. "Don't take me home," she said. "I'm not going there tonight."

Adam turned the car around and headed for his house.

"My entire family is staying with me. There's no telling what I'll admit if I have to continually be hugged and congratulated," Teddy said. "And believe me they will want every detail that a newly engaged person should know."

"I apologize," Adam said as they walked into his house. He turned the light on in the living room and Teddy went in.

Nothing about their situation was black-and-white. There were too many shades of gray, too many shadows that hadn't been lighted.

Teddy sat down heavily. Adam came to her and sat facing her on the sofa table. He took her hands.

"I'm sorry," he apologized again. "I never told my mother we were engaged."

"Then where did she get the idea?"

"We were talking about Veronica like I told you. Remember where we were when you and Diana met us that day?"

Teddy thought a moment, wondering how that could matter. "It was on Nassau Street near the sandwich shop."

"We were standing in front of Varrick's Jewelry."

Teddy frowned. "So?"

"Veronica told my mother I was looking at wedding

rings. She jumped to conclusions. Then everything got out of hand."

"What are we going to do now?" Teddy asked. "An engagement wasn't part of the deal."

"It doesn't change anything. We know we're not really engaged."

"Adam, it changes everything," Teddy said in frustration. "Don't you see? Our parents are so happy. We made them happy with this…" she faltered "…with this false engagement. It's going to break their hearts when we split. If we'd just been going out together, even exclusively, the split doesn't have the same impact. But someone you're engaged to, someone you pledge your heart to enough to want to walk down the aisle with, that's a completely different level."

"Well, if we don't make a big deal of it, they can't. And they aren't with us every day, so they won't really be involved."

"Didn't you hear my mother as we left tonight? She wants me to email her a photo of the ring as soon as I get one."

"We can do that."

"Adam, we're not getting a ring."

Teddy was working herself into a frenzy. She wished this episode was over. She wished she'd never agreed to this plan. Christmas couldn't come fast enough for her.

Adam moved from the table to the sofa. He hugged her close. Teddy leaned against him, turning her face into his shoulder. His arms hugged her tighter. Teddy's head was pounding. She closed her eyes and tried to relax, tried to let the events of the day float away as if they had the substance of dreams. But she knew they didn't. They were as anchored to the earth as the Empire State Building.

"We can stick to the original plan," Adam whispered above her head.

"We didn't account for things well enough," she said. Her voice was low and sleepy. "From the very beginning we didn't have all the information we needed."

"What was that?" Adam asked.

"Our mothers already knew each other."

"They belong to the same sorority," Adam said.

"It's more than that." Teddy pulled back, out of his embrace. She slipped her feet out of her five-inch heels and tucked them up on the sofa. Hugging her knees she looked at him. God, he was gorgeous. "Things got too complicated. It seemed like a simple plan. That was the problem. It was *too* simple. We didn't think about the after."

"After?" Adam questioned.

"After we broke up. After we told our parents that we were no longer a couple. We didn't consider their feelings. Who knew the families would get together, that they would bond so quickly or at all. After ten minutes it was like they'd known and *liked* each other since childhood. But now, when we part…" She stopped, not wanting to think about that, but also not wanting Adam to know the kind of effect he had on her. "When we part, it's going to cause a rift."

"I can't dispute that." He paused, then stared at Teddy for so long she felt scrutinized, felt he was trying to commit everything about her to memory. Maybe he was thinking of the time when they wouldn't be constantly together. Teddy admitted she enjoyed being with him. Thinking of not seeing him again was like cutting off her arm. Hugging her knees tighter, Teddy made sure her arm was still intact.

"I have another plan," Adam said.

Teddy tensed. She looked at him with hard eyes. "Need I remind you that the first plan was your idea? Look where that's gotten us."

"It has you sitting in my living room with your shoes off and your feet up, looking every bit the confident woman you are. We'll get through this," he continued. "I promise."

Teddy hoped he could keep that promise. Skepticism must have been on her face, because Adam renewed his promise.

"Come here," he said.

She lowered her feet to the floor and went into his open arms. Teddy felt safe there. She felt as if he could make everything all right. That he could keep his promise.

"What will your parents think if you don't come home tonight?"

Teddy sat up straight. "Oh," she said, her hand going to her breasts. "I never asked if I could spend the night. I don't want to presume."

Adam stopped her. "You can spend the night."

"I'm sure my parents will be okay with this. They might even expect it. After all, we were engaged tonight."

"That's very progressive of them."

Teddy laughed against his chest.

"What?" he asked.

"It's not that they're progressive. You're the one who's old-fashioned."

"I am not." After a second, he added, "Why would you think that?"

"My parents lived together for three years before they got married. I'm sure in that time, they had sex and slept in the same bed."

"Ah, but did their parents know?"

She smiled. "I don't think they ever actually walked in on them, but pre–cell phones and pre-email and pre–caller ID, I'm sure one of them answered the phone when the other parent called. And barring all that, Thanksgiving dinner would be a clear giveaway when family comes to stay and finds toothbrushes, shoes and clothes hanging in the closet that don't belong to their child."

"We don't have any of that," he said.

She looked up at him. "No," she said, her voice conveying her feelings. "We don't."

Adam bent down and kissed her. Teddy should be used to him touching her tenderly. She should also be used to knowing that he could unleash an animal so ferocious it devastated her. That's what he was doing now. His mouth changed. His lips tantalized, promised, worked magic on her. Teddy could feel the prickly electricity that accompanied his touch.

His hands moved over her, skimming over her arms and finding the zipper at the back of her dress. He didn't immediately pull it down. His hands played over the fabric as his mouth sought and found the skin of her neck. Teddy gasped at the sensation that pulsed through her at his touch.

Her inner body responded, becoming aroused by the movement of his hands. They captured her curves, running down her body as if it was his and he needed to learn each indentation, every soft contour of the skin that covered her. Skin that was burning with anticipation. Fire burst inside her.

Teddy grew bold. Her hands touched Adam. He was covered. His shirt long-sleeved. His pants over long legs. Teddy began a crusade to remove them. Reaching for the first button, she slid it through its hole. One by one, she released them, freeing the shirt and exposing his chest. Her hands went inside it finger by finger. Skimming them over the skin, she felt the moisture the building heat was rendering. Bowing her head, Teddy pressed her lips to his nipple. It was hot, searing hot. Her tongue came out and she tasted him. He groaned, both holding her and pushing her back. Then, in an immeasurable amount of time, Adam's hands caught her head and pulled her mouth to his.

His tongue slipped inside, joining her, mating with her, sweeping deep into her mouth and holding her until breath demanded they part.

"I need you," he said, his voice so deep Teddy could only understand it because she had entered the same private world where the language was known by only the two of them.

"I know," she said. "I need you, too."

Pinning her to the sofa, Adam stretched out over

her. His body moved over her, working her dress up to her knees and then higher. His mouth devoured hers. Hands raked her sides, slid down her breasts. His mouth moved to her neck and her shoulders. The clothes were too much of a barrier. Teddy needed to, had to, get rid of them.

"Now," she said.

Adam reached under her dress and removed her stockings and panties. In a flash of speed, he stood, pulling her up. Her zipper was dispensed with, and her dress dropped to the floor. Teddy pushed the shirt over his shoulders and down his arms. It fell away. In the half light, she looked at his form. Her hands sculpted him, created him. First bones, then muscle, sinew, skin. Pouring on the color of dark brandy, she painted his arms, his shoulders, his belly. She angled into his tight waist and followed over the curves of his hips and butt until she reached his strong legs and feet. Then she circled his erection. Not an inch of his frame had been left to chance. She caressed him, covered all of him.

His body was hard and ready. She ran her hands over him, feeling the throb of blood that rushed to her hands. His hands tightened on her, squeezed her back as desire stormed through him. His mouth opened and his hands moved like speed demons over her flesh. The heat generated called for second-degree burns.

Together they fell from the sofa to the soft carpet. Adam pushed the coffee table aside and quickly they removed the last of their clothing. Like the opposite poles of a magnet, they snapped-moved together, returning to the positions they had before. Adam pulled a condom from his pants pocket and quickly covered himself. Then he reached for her. His massive body covered her as his erection penetrated her.

"Sweet," Teddy moaned, holding the word for an interminable amount of time. It was the sweetest feeling, the entry point. The center of her being and Adam had found it. He pushed into her until there was no more of him to give. Then he started the race. It was slow and easy, belying the pulsating rapture that it created. Blood raced through her at a pace equal to the sensations rioting within her.

Linking her fingers to his, Adam stretched them over her head. He dragged her upward, pulling her with him as they reached the limit of their horizontal height. He thrust into her, hard and fast. Like a drum, the rhythmic sound of percussion set them off. Teddy heard it in her head. Connecting with the beat, she worked with it, allowed it to lead her, fill her. She worked with the sound, keeping time with it. As the sound roared and the tempo increased, she exerted a greater effort. It was faster and faster, as if some insane drummer was setting the pace. Inside her the world was erupting. Bright rivers of passion pushed her on, egged her forward and upward, taking her to heights previously unreachable.

Hunger led her, forced her to go one more round, then another until she was unable to stop the shattering rhythm they'd set. Teddy thrashed and writhed under Adam, her body working at a demonic pace. Sounds ripped from her as she grunted with each fierce shock wave that seduced her body. The beast was within her, taking over. It was huge, hungry, with an undeniable need. It wanted more. It wanted it all. She wanted it all.

The explosion came. Her voice joined Adam's in an all-consuming cry of release. They collapsed on each other. The sound of ragged breath filled the room. Neither tried to be quiet. They needed air and each dragged it into their lungs as if they'd been on a planet without oxygen and had quickly returned to the earth.

Adam still lay on Teddy. Both were soaking wet. Both were still trying to get their breath to return to normal. Teddy felt the coolness of the room's air. The fiery equator of heat was subsiding. Adam shifted off her, a low groan escaping him.

"Each time," he began, needing to take a breath between each syllable, "each time we're together, I don't think it can get any better. And then it does."

Chapter 8

Adam now had clothes at Teddy's house. She couldn't leave his house wearing the dress she'd had on for Thanksgiving. She wore a pair of his shorts and a T-shirt with Invest Now written across the front. Teddy didn't know what time her family got in, but when she quietly opened the door just after sunrise, the house was still quiet.

She went to her room and quickly changed into jeans and a sweater. After her morning ritual of brushing her teeth and cleaning her face, she made sense of her hair and went to the kitchen to begin breakfast. No one showed up for another hour. Teddy was on her second cup of coffee by then and knew today would be at least a three—if not four—cup day.

"You're up early," her father said, coming into the kitchen."

"Breakfast?" she asked.

"That bacon sure smells good," he said.

"You can have one slice," Teddy told him. "Mom said so."

"I guess she's been giving orders already."

"You know Mom," Teddy teased.

Teddy made breakfast and one by one her family showed up.

"Did you enjoy the party yesterday?" her father asked. He was right in the middle of things, but pretended like the party was news to him.

"I had a wonderful time," Sienna said.

"Planning to see Galen again?" Teddy asked. She was teasing her sister, hoping they wouldn't get into any discussion about Adam and her. And the wicked engagement blunder that had set off a hailstorm of fear within her.

"Not sure," Sienna said. "But I'm sure Mother will let you know."

Conversation at the table reviewed the uneventful events of Thanksgiving. But then Gemma Granville came to the table and the dynamics changed.

"I'll fix you a plate," Teddy told her mom.

"It's all right, I can get it."

The room was full of happy voices. Teddy's mom took a place and made her own breakfast. They sat around the table for nearly an hour.

"I have to go or I'm going to miss my plane," Sienna said.

Traveling activity filled the house with each of her siblings getting their suitcases and travel bags.

"What time is your flight?" Teddy asked Sienna.

"I have a ride," she said.

"With who?" Teddy asked.

Sienna only smiled. "He'll be here soon and I need to go put my makeup on."

Sienna didn't need any makeup and rarely wore much. Teddy was in no doubt that Galen would be arriving to pick her up.

As it turned out, Teddy didn't have to take anyone to the airport or train station. Apparently, they'd all made arrangements for themselves. She waved goodbye and hugged her sisters and brother as they climbed into a car that Galen Sullivan was driving and headed to the airport.

Forty minutes later, her parents were climbing into their SUV for the trip home.

"Mom, did I hear you say the painting was wrong?"

Gemma Granville nodded. "You didn't look at it?"

"When he brought it out, it was already packaged and ready to go. Not that I would know it wasn't the right one anyway. You never told me what it was a picture of."

"I'm sorry, but don't worry about it. I've made arrangements to go to the city and do some Christmas shopping. I'll return it and get the right one."

Teddy thought she was going to get away without a discussion related to the engagement, but she should have realized that was a fool's logic.

"Have you and Adam thought about a wedding date?" her mother asked from her seat in the SUV.

"We only got engaged less than twelve hours ago."

"June is a good month," her mother said as if Teddy had given her a date.

"You realize it takes a year to plan a wedding. June is an extremely popular month. We could be talking about a year from June."

"You're in the business, Teddy. I'm sure you won't have to wait that long. Call in some favors." Her mother waved away her argument as if it meant nothing. "I'll tell you what. I'll come up in a couple of weeks and we'll begin planning it."

"Mom, I have four weddings this month. I won't have time for another one. Why don't we make it after Christmas?"

Teddy knew the entire business would be over before any planning was necessary.

Her mother looked as if she was thinking this over. "I suppose that would be better," she agreed. "I'll just book the church and the reception. Think I can do that with a couple of phone calls."

"Don't, please." There was pleading in Teddy's voice. "Adam and I need to discuss it first. Then I promise, we'll give you a date and you can go crazy with details."

That seemed to placate her. Her smile was huge. She reached through the window and gave Teddy a tight hug.

"Bye, dear."

"Bye." Teddy waved to her father and he backed down the driveway.

She should be angry with Adam for putting her in this predicament, but she couldn't. She remembered last night. And if an engagement could result in that, they should get engaged more often.

Teddy loved her family, but she was so glad to see them go. Her mother and sisters extracted a promise from her to send them photos of the engagement ring as soon as she got it.

By Monday, Teddy had spent two days washing sheets, towels, clearing away dishes and restoring her home to the place where she lived. The city was in full shopping mode. Roads were constantly clogged with drivers in pursuit of Christmas bargains. Getting anywhere on time was purely coincidental.

It was also a busy time for Weddings by Diana. Teddy had four weddings in December. And there was the annual winter fashion show that the office sponsored. In the beginning, she and Diana established two shows a year to bring in business. The two had morphed into huge events with SRO attendance and sales to match.

The van was packed and ready for her and Diana. Renee and several other associates left yesterday to get everything set up and ready. Only two people would remain in the office and Teddy should also be gone, but she was still in her office going over the final details, searching for a particular veil that Renee had called and asked her to bring.

"Have we got everything?" Diana asked, coming in. She was holding a dress bag needed for the fashion show.

"I thought everything was in the van." Teddy indicated the bag.

"This is a surprise," Diana said. Then noticing Teddy fumbling through things, she asked, "What are you looking for?"

"The clover veil." Teddy pulled a drawer opened and shuffled the contents aside. Then she closed it and looked in another drawer. It wasn't there, either. Leaving her office, she went to search Renee's. She found the veil in the third drawer, already in a box with a label on it. She returned to her office.

"The keys," she said to herself. "Where did I put the keys?"

"I'll drive," Diana said, lifting them from beneath a pile of fabric samples. "You appear to be in no condition."

Teddy wasn't. She didn't argue with her partner. "I'm sorry. I just have a lot of details on my mind." She knew Diana had seen her stressed before, but not this stressed. It wasn't the work. It was Adam and their engagement. How could she go and fall in love with him? How could she fake the engagement?

The two headed outside and climbed into the SUV bearing the logo for Weddings by Diana. Diana put the vehicle in gear and drove out of the driveway. The fashion show was taking place in New Brunswick, less than an hour away if traffic didn't slow them down. Neither woman said a word until Diana pulled onto

Route 27 and headed north. At this hour the interstates would take a long time to reach and be packed when they got to them.

"Teddy, you're obviously tense. What happened? You said Thanksgiving went well, but I'm thinking that wasn't how it actually turned out."

Teddy leaned her head back and closed her eyes for a moment. "Adam asked me to marry him."

"What!" Diana took a long glance at her.

"In front of everyone. My sisters and brother. His brothers. Both sets of parents. I couldn't say no. My mother and his mother stood in front of us practically panting for me to accept the proposal. I thought they were going to hug and jump up and down like happy children when I said yes." She glanced at Diana. "Then they did just that."

"You said yes?" Diana nearly screamed.

Teddy nodded. "There was nothing else I could do."

"Teddy, I thought this was a temporary arrangement."

"It is," Teddy said, but she wasn't sure anymore.

Diana lowered her voice. It was compassionate. She understood part of what Teddy was feeling. "What happens now?"

"I don't know. We haven't figured that out yet."

"When was the last time you talked to Adam?"

"Friday morning." It was when she left his bed, but she kept that tidbit of information to herself.

The phone rang and Teddy automatically punched the media button on the Bluetooth phone then spoke into the air. She listened for a few seconds. "You're kidding?" she said.

More time passed. Teddy listened again. Diana watched anxiously.

"What about Grace?" Teddy asked whoever was on the other end of the line.

"Never mind. I'll handle it when I get there."

Irritated, she hung the phone up.

"What's wrong," Diana asked.

"Brianna caught a cold. She won't be able to model. And Renee has no substitutes for her."

Diana looked at the dress bag. "She has a lot of outfits."

"And they're already at the hall. Renee said they tried to find a replacement, but no one is available." Teddy put a hand to her temples and squeezed. She'd had a headache since Thanksgiving. It didn't help that this show was adding to her stress, and now she had no one to model a huge collection of gowns.

"You and Brianna are the same size. And you were one of the first models—"

"No," Teddy said.

"We have to have someone model the gowns. She's got some of the best of your creations and the back-stage dressing and getting ready will be totally off if someone doesn't fill in."

"Can anything else go wrong today?" Teddy asked rhetorically.

Diana looked at her and smiled. "Adam could show up."

* * *

The snow didn't last long. The temperature climbed into the mid-fifties melting all vestiges of it away two days after Thanksgiving. By the day of the fashion show, the township was shades of winter gray and brown, but the holiday lights swinging from every streetlight and lamp pole gave the place a festive look.

"What are we doing here?" Quinn asked Adam. The two men had gotten out of Adam's car and headed for the door. Quinn saw the sign announcing the fashion show. "I get it. Teddy must be here."

"She is."

"Can't the two of you be without the other for a few hours."

"We can, but why should we?"

"You know this place will be full of women?"

"When did that ever bother you?" Adam asked.

"When they are already engaged."

The two men went inside. Not only was there to be a fashion show, but a trade show was also in progress. Everything anyone could want or need for a wedding was on display. Adam and Quinn passed china, cookware, photographers, invitations, florists, bakeries and jewelers. Even Realtors, furniture stores and design firms were represented.

Quinn stopped him in front of one display. Adam looked down. Trays of engagement rings gleamed brilliantly against a black velvet background.

"How about that one?" Quinn pointed to a platinum setting with a large stone perched on top of it. It appeared to be floating in the sea of black.

"I've been told to never buy an engagement ring without the bride's approval."

"Who said that?"

"I did."

Both turned to find Veronica standing there.

"The last time we met, you were standing in front of a jeweler," she told Adam. "Hello, Quinn."

"Veronica, this is a surprise. What are you doing here?" Quinn asked.

She laughed. "Obviously you've never been to one of these shows."

"Guilty," he said.

"Newlyweds want newness in their lives. They are into decorating. Anything from an apartment to a mansion is open to change. And I'm a decorator." In her hand was a stack of business cards and flyers. "Our booth is over there." She pointed to the end of the row. "The other financial managers are at the end of that row next to the wedding gowns and tuxedo groups. You guys got the best location. Everyone goes for the gowns."

"Financial managers?" Adam questioned.

"Isn't that why you're here?" She raised her perfectly arched eyebrows. "People are looking at their long-term financial goals earlier and earlier." She swung her gaze between the two men. "You mean you're not here to gain potential clients?"

"We're here for the fashion show," Adam said.

"I hope you have tickets."

"Tickets?" Quinn said.

Veronica laughed. "You guys are so out of your element."

Renee was equipped with pins, buttons, tape measure, needle and thread, and extras of everything. She had to take over for Teddy, who had to take over for their model Brianna.

"You look stunning," Renee told Teddy, who stepped back and admired the wedding gown she was wearing.

Teddy took a long breath. She wasn't afraid of the runway. She'd been on plenty of runways, although not in the past few years. The mirror in front of her reflected her image. Teddy tried to smile at the tall, thin woman who'd been her right hand for the past three years.

"Renee, you've seen hundreds of brides."

"I've never seen you in a gown, only that one picture that used to hang in your office at the other location."

That photo had been of Teddy in the gown she'd modeled for Diana and sold right off her back. Every now and then she wondered about the woman who bought it and if she was still happily married.

"How much time do we have?" Teddy asked, slipping a ring on her finger. It was a faux diamond engagement ring similar to the ones the other models wore.

"About ten minutes. Practically all the seats are taken. If we can get through the chaos back here, the show should go fine."

It was always chaotic behind the scenes of the fashion show, but every year it turned out fine. Teddy clung to that thought. Diana would act as emcee as she always did.

Teddy saw Diana coming. She was walking fast and her face showed the stress Teddy felt. Something else had obviously gone wrong.

"I'm going to check the stage one more time," Renee said. There was a full crew taking care of it, but Renee was a detail person and she would make sure everything was fine before she returned to be the dresser for Teddy and three other models.

"Ready?" Teddy asked Diana.

"I need the train pulled up," she said.

Diana turned around. Teddy found the loop in the middle of the train and pulled it up to the third button on the back. She looped it twice to secure it.

"There," Teddy said.

"Now I can turn around without tripping or kicking the dress."

Teddy knew she was teasing. The dress was one of Teddy's designs. It was a new one. Diana always wore a new design for the show.

"Time to start," Diana said.

Teddy turned for one last check in the mirror. She was the third gown out.

"There's one more thing I think you should know," Diana said.

"What's that?" This was the real reason her friend had come over.

"Remember on the drive here, when you asked if anything else could go wrong today?"

Teddy nodded. Her breath suddenly died, and then she was heaving for air.

"He's in the audience. Last row on the right."

Teddy stepped onto the runway. Bright lights blinded her, but she didn't squint and didn't look to the last row on the right. With a smile on her face, she concentrated on Diana's voice as she described the gown. Teddy pivoted and turned on cue at the end of the extrawide runway. Using her hand, she swirled the train up and around to the unexpected gasp of appreciation from the audience.

She displayed the dress for about a minute before she headed to the back and exited through the curtain that raised as she approached it. Teddy went left. The next model entered from the right.

Teddy exhaled with a hand on her breasts as her knees grew weak. Adam was indeed in the house. Renee rushed over to help her down the three steps and into the dressing area.

"What's he doing here?" she muttered to herself.

While she hadn't looked directly at him, Teddy noticed Adam and his brother. She wasn't sure if it was Quinn or Galen.

Renee immediately started releasing the buttons on the gown and getting the next dress she was to model.

"Do we have any financial investment companies in the trade show?" Teddy asked.

"We have some financial planners from big firms. So yes."

That must be why he was here, Teddy thought. But why didn't he tell her he was coming?

She stepped out of the gown and someone whisked it away to rehang it in the numbered bag that corresponded to its order number. Teddy stepped into the next gown and Renee zipped and buttoned her in. Another associate wrapped the veil around the crown of her head. Teddy could have been a robot. She raised her arms when told, lifted her feet and stepped into shoes, bowed her head for veils, and closed her eyes or opened them for makeup. Her mind wasn't on dressing.

It was on Adam.

Adam was president of his investment firm. Someone else could be in charge of sales and not mentioned this particular trade show. Or not mentioned it by name. She looked for excuses for him, for a reason he'd be here.

And Thanksgiving, that disastrous day, had provided such an unexpected turn of events that thinking about a trade show couldn't have been on the top of his mind.

Twelve other models had gone up the steps and back in the time it took for Teddy to change. She went to the edge of the curtain and waited. Then she moved into the center space. Her train was adjusted so it would drag behind her in a perfectly straight line. Her veil covered her face giving her a small sense of invisibility and allowing her to look in Adam's direction.

The curtain rose. She stood there a second. The audience applauded. Teddy stole a glance at Adam. His smile had her heart lurching. Clinging more tightly to the fresh flowers in her hands and mentally counted the steps she went through before returning to the dressing room.

"Teddy, don't crush the flowers," Renee admonished as she took the bouquet. "We want to use them more than once."

Teddy hadn't noticed the flowers. They were donated by one of the florists participating in the trade show. Looking at them, she was surprised to see the mangled stems. Renee took a towel and cleaned her hands of the green stains.

Teddy followed the routine four more times, careful to keep from destroying the bouquets. She checked Adam's position each time and never once did he move. She wondered if something had happened. Was he waiting for her to be free to tell her something, like maybe he'd confessed their deception to his parents? Or he'd taken one of his brothers in confidence and they spilled the beans? One unwelcome scenario after another ran through her mind.

Her cell phone was on silent and carefully tucked away in her purse. She wondered if there was a message from her mother. She wondered if Veronica, whom she'd seen immediately after entering the building, had somehow lured Adam here. Telling herself she was being paranoid, Teddy concentrated on not tripping over her feet.

"Last one," Renee said, breaking into her thoughts as she placed the last gown over her head. "After this there's the finale."

The words should have made her feel better. The

show was coming to an end, but Teddy knew when it was over, there might be bad news on the other end.

"Teddy?" Renee called to her.

Teddy was standing in front of a three-way mirror that had been brought in for the models. She looked at Renee. The other woman looked confused.

"What is it?" Teddy asked.

Renee had swept Teddy's hair to the side and anchored it with an S-shaped rhinestone clip that had veil netting attached to it. The veil didn't cover her face, but hung down the side of her head balancing the asymmetrical shape of the dress bodice.

Teddy adjusted the veil.

"You're very distracted today," Renee said. "Is everything all right? Diana told me to keep this one as a surprise for you. That you'd love it. But you barely looked at it."

Teddy looked down and screamed, her hands going to her mouth and cutting off the sound.

"I don't understand," Teddy said. "Where did she find this?"

"Is it all right?" Concern entered Renee's voice. "What's wrong?"

"Nothing, nothing." Teddy lowered her voice to a calming level. She placed her hand on Renee's arm to assure her. "I just wasn't expecting this."

"What is it?"

"The first wedding gown I ever designed and sold." Teddy turned all the way around, looking at the way the dress moved. She took a few dance steps. When she'd conceived the idea, she'd wanted to make sure the bride's grown swayed like those of a professional dancer. She stopped and looked at herself again. It was perfect.

"This is the one from the picture," Renee said. "I almost didn't recognize it. It's so much prettier in person."

"Where did Diana find this?"

"She didn't say. Only that it was a surprise." Renee straightened one side and admired Teddy in the glass. "It's beautiful. When I get married, I want one of your designs."

"It'll be my present to you." Teddy smiled and squeezed Renee's shoulder.

Renee beamed, then continued her duties. "Time to get you on stage."

Teddy went through the curtain. A chorus of oohs and ahhs came from the audience, and then a long moment of applause. Teddy glanced at Diana with a smile on her face. In the audience she saw the owner of the gown who gave her a thumbs-up signal.

Teddy began the final walk, holding her head a little higher. This time her smile wasn't plastered on her face. It was genuine. Her groom, in this case it was Diana's husband, Scott, who'd been commandeered to play one of the male models, offered his arm and escorted her down the aisle. After she finished showing the gown, he took her to her final place in front of the chapel setting that had been erected for the finale.

She felt good in the dress. This is the way she wanted to feel on her wedding day, dressed in a gown of her own design and heading for the man she loved. Her eyes went directly to Adam when that thought came. Again he smiled at her and Teddy's insides did a meltdown. Scott gripped her arm tighter and she steadied. The other models finished their routines and at the end they stood as a fifteen-bride wedding party, each woman with her groom. Teddy imagined the picture they presented.

As each of the models took her place in the finale line ending her presentation, thunderous applause erupted in the hall. The brides remained as they were, everyone smiling. Teddy knew they were relieved that the show was over, but also proud that it had gone over without too many glitches, all of which were backstage. The hired photographer and many of the guests took pictures.

Adam and his brother—she now recognized him as Quinn—came forward, each with a cell phone snapping photo after photo. Teddy wanted to leave, but she was trapped until the last camera flashed and the last question was answered. Adam didn't ask any questions. He stood with his arms crossed and watched and waited.

Why wasn't he at his station, talking to people about investing in their future? Why was he remaining in the background, like a suitor waiting for his bride? They both knew that despite his actions on Thanksgiving, the two were not engaged and not likely to be.

Traditionally, when the show ended, the models kept the finale gown on as they mingled with the crowds, allowing the crowd to see the designs and imagine how they would look in the dress. There was an information and order desk with forms, business cards and brochures about the wedding planning services. Brides could also make appointments for fittings or consultant services.

Normally Teddy and Diana would remain at the desk after the show while the consultants packed everything up. Today, both worked the room, leaving the job to two other consultants who'd volunteered for the duty.

As the models left the stage, Adam came forward and took Teddy's hand. His brother was behind him.

"You look beautiful," Adam whispered. He pulled her into his arms and kissed her on the cheek. Teddy was nervous. Why, she didn't know. When he pushed back, his hand went down her arm and lifted her hand. The faux diamond ring gleamed there. His eyes came to hers and she saw the question in them.

"We all wear rings," she explained. "After all, the bride is engaged." Teddy regretted the words as soon as they fell.

Quinn excused himself to look at the trade show. "He's really going to look at the models," Adam said when he was gone. "Are they all engaged?"

"A couple. The others are mainly models we hired for the day."

"Why are you modeling?"

"One of the models is ill. We're the same size. I stood in because she had some of the newest gowns and without them there would have been a large hole in the presentation." She paused for a moment. "And Diana talked me into it."

He nodded and dropped her hand.

Teddy felt a coldness settle in when he was no longer connected to her. "Shouldn't you be at your booth, talking to prospective clients?"

"We don't have a booth here. But if I'd known there would be this many people interested in investments, I'd have passed the idea on to Marketing."

Her brows rose. "If you're not here on business, why *are* you here?"

"We haven't talked since Thanksgiving," he said. "And that day didn't turn out the way we expected. I wanted to make sure you were all right."

"So you came here." Teddy spread her hands.

"So I came here," he said. "To this female dominated den where people are talking about crystal, lace and honeymoon destinations."

The crowd around them pressed closer, forcing them to step closer to each other. Teddy could smell Adam's cologne. The heady scent reminded her of when their bodies were separated by nothing but sexual desire.

Her heartbeat increased. She was jostled from behind, pushing her into Adam's arms. Even without the push she was already about to hug him.

"I know we're not really engaged," she whispered. "But you coming here, to a place you said you don't want to be, is the most romantic thing anyone has ever done for me."

Adam pushed her back and Teddy knew she was

about to be kissed, but he was stopped by a voice behind them.

"You two make a lovely couple. I can only imagine what your real wedding will be like."

Adam kept his arm around her waist as they turned to see Veronica.

"Congratulations." She glanced at Teddy's hand. "Beautiful ring."

Teddy raised her hand. Both she and Adam stared at the large stone. Neither of them corrected Veronica. She wanted to know what Adam was thinking, what he was feeling. Teddy was the one supposedly engaged to Adam, yet her heart felt as if there was a tear in it. When their camouflage ended, who would Adam seek out? Was he ready to take the risk again? Had Teddy made him see that he could love again?

"Have you set a date yet?" Veronica asked.

"Not yet," Adam said.

"Well, congratulations again." Veronica looked at Teddy as if she'd lost a prize. But Teddy knew *she* was the one who'd lost.

Chapter 9

Teddy flopped on the sofa, tired from the exertion of helping Adam carry a gargantuan pine tree from the garage to his condo.

"Why did you have to park so far from the door?" she asked, out of breath.

"You're not that much out of shape." He turned from leaning the tree against the wall next to the fireplace and looked at her. "You're not out of shape at all."

"Well, I'm used to running and lifting weights, not carrying awkwardly shaped objects that stab my hands and face with needles."

"Remember, this was your idea," Adam reminded her. "And you only carried it from the car."

"I might regret it before this is over."

"I don't think so," he said.

Teddy heard the need in his voice. Earlier she'd commented on the lack of Christmas decorations in his condo. When she was young and all her siblings lived with their parents, they always put their tree up right after Thanksgiving. Teddy asked where he kept them, and she was surprised to learn he had none. It was her idea that they go shopping. Together they bought a tree, a world of colorful bulbs and lights, a garland for the fireplace, and an assortment of ornaments.

Adam put on some Christmas music and Teddy went to the kitchen. She poured two cups of apple cider and warmed them in the microwave. When she got back to the living room, Adam was lighting the fireplace. The condo had all the modern touches and supported a glass-enclosed built-in structure that burned gas and could be lit with a match. It sat high on the wall and produced no smoke and no fumes.

Adam accepted the cup and took a sip. He set it on an end table and attacked the many boxes and bags littering the floor. Finding the tree stand, he worked quickly to set it up. Teddy opened the bags and organized the contents into sections: lights, ornaments, angel for the top, timers, extension cords, tree skirt, garlands and more. Even with organization, the room was strewn with discarded store bags and boxes.

"I think we overbought," Adam said.

Teddy shook her head. She watched as Adam worked. For a long moment she couldn't take her eyes off him. He had his back to her and she was free to stare at him. His arms were strong under the sweater he wore. It filled out his form and Teddy was in no doubt of the muscles it concealed. She wanted them around her.

"There," Adam said. He shook the tree to make sure it was sitting in the stand and held sturdy enough that it wouldn't fall over. He turned to Teddy. "Your turn."

"This is a group effort," she told him. "We decorate together." She handed him a box. "Lights first."

As they moved back and forth and around the tree for the next hour, the decorations quickly disappeared from their boxes, turning the tree into a brightly lit work of art. A garland of pine branches was arranged around the fireplace. The holiday cards he'd stacked on a table were tucked in the garland they hung around the room's entry. Adam moved his cup and interspersed the table with scented candles and several Santa Claus statues. Teddy lit the candles and the fragrance of Christmas cookies permeated the air.

"That's it." Adam stood back and checked their work. Dropping down on the sofa, he checked the boxes still unopened. "We did overbuy."

"We're not finished," Teddy said. Taking his hand, she pulled him up. He came forward, his arms going around her waist as his body came in contact with hers. Teddy looked up as his head swooped down and he kissed her. Teddy wanted to stay in his embrace. She raised her arms and circled his neck. For a long moment the kiss went on. Her knees weakened and she forced herself to push back.

"We need to keep our heads," she said.

"I have my head," he said, kissing her again. "It's your head that I'm working on."

"We have to finish these," she insisted.

"I thought we *were* finished."

Teddy moved back. "This room is done, but there are other rooms."

"We decorate the entire condo?"

"Didn't you ever do this when you were younger?"

"We decorated the family room, where the tree was. In the kitchen, Mom put out some red-and-green dish towels, but that was it."

Teddy picked up a small lighted tree from a box.

"Where is that going?"

"Follow me."

She went into his bedroom.

"I was wondering how I was going to get you in here."

Teddy shot him a warning glance. "Bring the small box with the Kwanzaa kinara," she told him. She set up the tree on a table and plugged it in. The white lights gave the room a soft glow. Adam came up behind her and put his arms around her waist. Kissing her neck, he set the candleholder next to the tree and gathered her close against him.

"Need anything more?" he asked.

"Not a single thing," she said. Sidestepping him, Teddy left the room and finished the decorations. She placed towels in the kitchen as Adam said his mom had done. In the dining room, she placed a red-and-gold runner on the table and set a basket of silver bells in the center. Ten minutes later, she looked around.

"Is everything done now?" Adam asked.

"All except plugging in the lights."

Back in the living room, Teddy turned off the room lights and took a seat. Adam threw the plug-strip switch and the tree lights blinked on.

Adam joined her, his arm along the back of the sofa and resting on her shoulder.

"You're right," he said.

"About what?"

"The decorations. I didn't know how much I missed them. Thanks for today, for shopping and helping me trim it."

Teddy looked up at him. In the subdued light of the tree, he was even more handsome. Her eyes rested on his mouth. Biting her lip, she tried to keep from moving toward him. She put her head on his shoulder, snuggled into his arm and faced the tree.

"It looks so much better than if you'd hired a decorator to do it," she said.

Adam's arm tightened on her shoulder as he helped her settle into his side. "I was thinking the same thing."

"Great minds…" They were a pair, Teddy thought with a smile. If only he felt the way she did. Teddy was quiet for a long time. She and Adam watched the fire and watched the tree. Previous conversations they'd had came to mind. But the Thanksgiving proposal was at the top.

"I have a question," Teddy said. She knew it was an inappropriate time to ask it, but she couldn't keep it in any longer. She was in his arms. She felt safe and warm and wanted to stay there, but she had to know.

"Shoot," Adam said.

"Remember when we had the conversation about meeting someone? Finding your one and only?"

She felt the arm about her stiffen. His entire body did the same, although she knew he was trying to control it. They were too close, too connected to each other.

"You've found someone?" His question was stated as distinct words, each one given equal weight, as if they needed to struggle to reach an audible sound.

"Not me," Teddy said. "I thought, since you ran into Veronica, you might have second thoughts about us." The impact of the word *us* hit her. It sounded as if they were a real couple and this was a defining moment in their relationship. She rushed on. "About what we're doing."

Adam put his hand under her chin and lifted it until she was looking in his eyes. "She's not my one and only."

Teddy didn't think she could hold the tears back, so she closed her eyes. She felt his lips brush hers and it turned into a kiss. Adam's hand combed through the hair above her ear as he kissed her deeply.

Varrick's Jewelry was founded the same year as Princeton University and had maintained its present location as the tiny college town grew to its present size. Teddy wondered how many graduates had crossed the main street in Princeton and bought an engagement ring in all the time the store had existed?

Adam opened the glass doors with gilded handles forming a V. The store housed some of the most beautiful jewelry in the world. Teddy pushed the door closed and stepped aside. She stood in front of one of the windows. Behind the glass was a diamond necklace. A huge stone was set at the center, completely surrounded by rubies. It was beautiful.

Teddy turned away from it. She didn't want Adam to see the awe on her face at beauty so exquisite it took her breath away.

"Adam, why are we here? There's only a few weeks left before we end this charade. I don't need an engagement ring."

"Your mother wants a photo and mine calls me nearly every day and asks if we've got the ring and have we set the date."

"I can wear that ring I had on at the fashion show. It's hard to tell the difference between that and a real diamond."

Adam frowned. "You don't think our mothers will be able to tell the difference?"

Teddy knew they would. "Not in a photograph and I'm sure I can avoid your mom for three more weeks. I'll be working several weddings in that time and I won't be available for visits."

"And when they show up on your doorstep, unannounced. What will you do then?"

"I'll think of something," Teddy told him. She knew it could happen. When her dad spoke at the symposium, that had been impromptu. Her father could have come alone as he often did when he went to speak at colleges. Her mother had come to Princeton to check on her and Adam.

"Why don't we just go in and look," Adam suggested. "We're already here."

That sounded a lot like the first dinner they had together. They ate because they were already at the restaurant. And look where that had led her.

Despite her protests Adam ushered Teddy inside. With all the holiday traffic, entering Varrick's was like finding a sanctuary. There were no crowds rushing past her, no frantic mothers vying for the hot toy of the season.

Teddy followed Adam. He went straight to the counter holding engagement rings as if he'd been there before. Then she remembered he had been married. But he was very young then and his business was new. She doubted he could have afforded a ring from Varrick's.

"Adam, I really don't need a ring." Even as she said it, Teddy looked in the case at the settings being displayed. She held her breath so she wouldn't gush over what she saw. "I'm sure we can tell our parents that we want to find the right one before committing. Or that you're planning to give it to me on Christmas. Since this will be over by then, we shouldn't go through buying one."

"If we don't choose a ring, they'll probably choose one for us, and tell us it's a wedding present. Like I said, let's just look. If you don't like anything, we can leave."

When they emerged an hour later, Teddy was wearing a square-cut flawless diamond engagement ring. It felt heavy and foreign on her hand. She knew she'd tried to talk Adam out of a ring altogether, but secretly she loved it. Even though their pretense wasn't going to last much longer and there was no reason for her to have a ring, especially one that was over five carats and cost enough to rival half of the inventory at Weddings by Diana. Still, Teddy loved it.

Adam took her hand and looked at the huge stone. "My mother would expect it and I'm sure yours will, too." He could practically read her mind.

Of course he was right. Teddy stared at it in the bright December sun. It was a gorgeous stone. And she liked the way it looked on her hand. It made her fingers appear long and elegant. She was going to be sorry to give it back.

"Why did you ask the jeweler if it could be returned?" Adam asked when they were on the street.

"You don't think I would keep it," she said, amazed that he thought she would. "Although it does look great on my hand." She stretched her fingers open. She'd done it at least fifty times since Adam lifted it and placed it on her finger. It wasn't like the one she'd worn for the fashion show. This was a real diamond. It had significance. It represented two people who wanted to live their lives together.

"Feeling like a bride?" Adam asked.

"I am," she said in surprise.

"Next time our parents show up, you can show them the ring."

"We won't have to wait for that," Teddy said.

Adam opened the door to his car and Teddy got inside.

"Why not?" he asked when he was seated and pulling out of a parking space that another car was waiting to take.

"My mother already called, asking if I'd chosen something and not to forget to send her a photo."

"So she knew you were getting a ring."

"She assumed."

Moments later Adam pulled the car into her driveway. "Looks like you won't need to send a photo," Adam said. "You have guests."

"I don't recognize the car," Teddy said.

"It belongs to *my* mother," Adam said. Stopping next to it, Teddy saw her mother in the passenger seat.

"Mom," she called. Teddy got out of the car and rushed around to greet her. "I thought you were—" Midway to where Gemma Granville stood, Teddy stopped. By the look on her mother's face Teddy knew something was wrong.

Thinking something might have happened to her dad, she rushed forward.

"What's wrong," she asked. "Dad? Is Dad all right?"

"This has nothing to do with your father."

"Sienna, Sierra—"

She put her hand up to stop Teddy from going through the full list of relatives. "Nothing to do with any of them. It's about you."

"And you." Adam's mother leveled her comment to him. The harshness of her words were enough to hold back a flood.

"How could you?" Gemma Granville said, with the slight hitch in her voice.

"How could I what?"

"Fake your engagement?"

The four of them stood in the crisp December air—speechless. Teddy fingered the ring on her finger, feeling like a child caught doing something wrong. Tension around them was like a chill factor, reducing the trust and love that had always been part of their collective lives. Teddy felt numb. How did they know?

"We'd better go inside and discuss this." Adam appeared to remain rational. He took Teddy's elbow and led her toward the door. Their parents followed.

Teddy found her key with some prompting. Adam took it and opened the front door. Warmth hit her as she led the small procession through the foyer and into the living room. The coldness of the outside was gone. She felt hot and tense. They sat facing each other, she and Adam on one side, their parents as accusers on the other.

"How did you find out?" Teddy asked her mother.

"As if that matters," she said. "Gene Restonson told us."

Teddy frowned. "Gene who?"

"The gallery owner in New York. Remember I told you I got the wrong painting? Well, Ann and I returned it today. And while I was telling Gene how romantically Adam proposed to you on Thanksgiving, he told us about you two agreeing to deceive us."

Teddy winced, remembering that conversation. She hadn't thought anyone could hear them. The gallery was empty. But when he brought the painting out, he was right behind her. It was unimportant now. Their parents knew the truth.

"I am so hurt and angry," her mother said. There was that hitch in her voice again. "Why did you two think you needed to lie to us?" She looked at Teddy, then at Adam and back again.

"Mom, we didn't really. You wanted us to like each other…and we do." Teddy glanced at Adam for confirmation. He took her hand in assurance, but it didn't seem to affect the two mothers. They sat across from them in individual chairs. Teddy had the feeling this was a court and she and Adam were on dual witness seats. The problem was they *were* guilty.

"We thought if you believed we were really getting close to each other, that you would stop…" She trailed off, not wanting to make matters worse by telling them to stop meddling.

"Go on," her mother said, raising her chin slightly. "What would we stop?"

"Sending us blind dates, commenting on our single status," Adam said.

"And you were so happy when I told you we were going to continue to see each other," Teddy explained.

"You think I, we—" she used her hand to encompass both Adam's mother and herself "—want you to be married so badly that you needed to fake a relationship?"

Teddy refused to answer. She held her mother's gaze but did not reply to the question.

"And what about that proposal on Thanksgiving?"

Adam's mother asked him. "Were you going to go as far as planning a fake wedding?"

"Of course we weren't," Adam replied. "We were going to break up just before Christmas. You'd be disappointed, but you'd stop with the marriage tests for a while."

"Mom," Teddy hesitated. "I'm sorry. I never meant to hurt you."

"Well, you have. The whole family, in fact. Your sisters were already talking about being bridesmaids. And even though your father never said it, he was glad you'd finally found someone to care for you."

"And I was thinking of finally being the mother of the groom," Ann Sullivan addressed them both. "I thought you'd be over Veronica and Chloe by now and ready to start a new life, but I see I was wrong."

Teddy looked at Adam. "Who's Chloe?" she asked.

Ann Sullivan froze. Teddy noticed her reaction, but the question went unanswered when Teddy's mother spoke.

"Can I take it you two are not in love with each other?" Gemma Granville asked. It took all the courage Teddy had to look at Adam. She didn't know what to say. She wanted him to answer first. She wanted to know why he'd told her about Chelsea and Veronica, even introduced her to the woman, but failed to mention anyone named Chloe.

"We're not," he finally said. His answer was for the two mothers, but his gaze never left Teddy's face.

Teddy felt a dagger plunge into her heart.

* * *

The two mothers looked as if they'd been shocked. Even if they were expecting confirmation, they weren't prepared for it. Dr. Sullivan stood up and Gemma Granville did the same.

"There's to be no wedding?" Gemma said.

Teddy shook her head. Her hands were in her lap. She'd pulled the one Adam was holding away when his eyes told her that his mother's comments were true. She felt the weight of the square-cut diamond on her third finger. She twisted it around so the stone wasn't visible.

"No wedding," Teddy said.

"Well," Dr. Sullivan said on a resigned sigh. "Then I'll be leaving." She turned to Gemma. "I'll see you later."

She went to the door and pulled it open. Adam stood up. "Mom," he called, but she continued walking, going out into the December afternoon. Moments later they heard her car start.

"Teddy, I'll call you later," he said over his shoulder as he, too, headed for the door.

Teddy got up and called him. She followed him into the foyer. At the door she took his arm to stop him. Immediately, she dropped her hand as if his touch burned. They watched his mother back down the driveway and drive away.

"Don't forget this." Teddy looked at the huge ring on her finger for several seconds. Then she pulled it off and handed it to him. "We only got it today. I'm sure they'll take it back."

"I need to go now, but this isn't over. I'll call you."

Adam quickly kissed her cheek and left. Teddy knew their show for the parents had become so natural that his kiss was still part of the charade. She couldn't see a need for further conversation. They hadn't wanted a relationship from the start. Now that everything was out in the open, there was no need to do anything except hope they could mend the open rift with their families.

She watched as the second car in her driveway exited and headed in the same direction as the previous one. Back in the living room, her mother was standing in the same spot.

"Can we talk?" Teddy asked.

"Is there anything more to say?"

"I'm sorry," Teddy began.

She could see emotions playing across her features, then disappear as a new one replaced the last.

"I know you're disappointed in me. But I had a good reason. At least, I thought I did. I love you and I only wanted to please you."

"You thought a fake romance would please me?"

"You were so happy when you thought we were dating. When Adam proposed, I thought your heart would jump out of your chest."

Her mother looked down at the floor, then back at Teddy. "I was. I thought you'd finally found the man of your dreams and instead of running everyone else's wedding, you could finally have your day."

Teddy moved to where her mother stood. Only a foot separated them. "That happened, Mom." She took a moment to swallow.

The expression on her mother's face turned from confusion to apprehension and finally to understanding.

"You *are* in love with him." She said it like a person struggling with a foreign language, and comprehension finally made all the words make sense.

Teddy nodded, unable to speak over the lump clogging her throat. "He doesn't know. It wasn't part of the plan. But it happened and there's nothing I can do about it."

Mother and daughter gazed at each other for a long moment. Then Gemma Granville pulled her daughter in her arms and held her as if she were a five-year-old who'd scraped her knee.

"Come on, let's make some tea," her mother said. "You can tell me all about it, starting at the beginning."

Two days later, Adam couldn't remember the details that followed the conversation with his mother and Teddy's. What was burned into his visual memory was that Teddy had asked who Chloe was and the question went unanswered.

Adam had told her about Veronica, told her he'd been married to Chelsea, but never had he mentioned that he'd been about to marry a second time. Teddy was honest with him, but he'd held back. The reason didn't matter. He was no longer hurt by Chloe. Just as Veronica was old news, Chloe had found her place in the far reaches of his mind. Her betrayal no longer stung. He had no feelings for her, yet he'd kept her a secret. Everyone did, except Quinn. Quinn would mention Chloe's name, but the rest of his family took their cues from Adam and never mentioned her. They all knew how hurt he'd been by her that they'd agreed to his unasked request to never mention her.

Sitting in his family room, he could see Teddy everywhere he looked, even on his phone. The image of her in the wedding gown at the fashion show came up when he selected her number. She smiled from the small screen, innocent of the news that would change her opinion of him forty-eight hours after that photo was snapped.

In his hand was the engagement ring he'd bought her. Despite what people said about diamonds being cold, he could feel the warmth, Teddy's warmth. He felt like a heel, an idiot, a jerk. Putting the ring on the table, he lifted his coffee mug and took a drink.

He told her he'd call. But he hadn't. It had been two days since he talked to her. Adam had opened his phone a hundred times and gone to her number, her photo, but he couldn't bring himself to press the call button. What could he say? Would she understand? Could he make her understand?

Staring at her photo, his heart ached. He never wanted to hurt Teddy, yet somehow he had. He'd broken her trust. It didn't matter that their relationship wasn't real. It didn't matter that they weren't really engaged or getting married. They had a deal. They'd made a pact and he'd held out on her.

Adam jumped as the phone in his hand rang. He expected Teddy's photo to disappear and the caller ID photo to show up, but it remained on the screen. It was *her*. Adam swallowed hard. He wanted to talk to

Teddy, but he wasn't ready. The phone rang a second time and a third. If he didn't answer now it would go to voice mail.

He pressed the answer button and said hello.

"Hi," Teddy said. Adam sat forward in the chair, pressing the phone closer to his ear. His heart was beating so fast he could hardly hear her. Yet the sound of her voice lifted his spirits.

"How are you?" he asked.

"I'd like to talk to you."

"I think that's a good idea. Should I come over?"

"No," she said.

"No?"

"I'm outside. Can I come in?"

Adam was at the window of his condo in a second. He looked down on the parking lot. Teddy looked up at him, holding her phone to her ear. He signaled for her to come up and immediately went to open the door.

When she entered the town house, he forced himself not to rush to her and gather her in his arms. She came inside and Adam took her coat, throwing it over the hall banister before leading her into the family room. The sun was setting and the room had become dark.

Teddy looked around. "The fire's dying," she said.

Adam didn't remember making a fire. He went to the hearth and added more of the liquid that burned the crystals. Sparks flew up but died quickly.

"I talked to my mother," Teddy said when he turned around. She was sitting on the sofa where he'd been only a few moments ago. "We're back to being friends. I told her everything." Teddy paused. Time stretched between them as if they were ex-lovers who hadn't seen each other in years and were at a loss for what to say after "hello." Teddy lifted his glass and took a sip of his coffee.

"I talked to mine, too. We're walking on eggshells."

"Do you think you'll work it out?"

"I'm going to try."

She smiled and he knew she approved. Teddy picked up the ring he'd left next to his coffee mug.

"I see you didn't return it," she said.

Adam shook his head.

"Why not?"

"No reason. I haven't been back to the store."

"But you are taking it back?" Teddy questioned.

Sitting down next to her, he said, "I've gotten us into a fine mess."

She nodded with a smile. "It's too bad we didn't just fall in love and make everything real."

Adam stared at her. He wanted to tell her that he had fallen in love with her, but her statement told him the love was one-sided.

"That would have solved all our problems." He paused a moment and took a drink. "But that didn't happen."

"No, it didn't."

He felt they were talking like two people who wanted to say something but were refusing to do so. He knew it was his turn to explain. Setting his mug on the table, he faced Teddy and took one of her hands.

"Chloe," he said, speaking only the one word.

Teddy waited.

"I should have told you about her."

"I understand that we didn't tell each other everything about our past. The point is moot now," she said. "Since the proverbial jig is up, I don't need to know."

Adam kept her hand in his. He ignored her comment. He wanted to tell her about Chloe. Other than Quinn, no one knew the whole story.

"It was a fairy-tale romance. We met at a picnic the year before I got out of college. Remember what that was like?"

Teddy nodded.

"Did you have a boyfriend that year?" he asked.

"Yes," she said, but didn't elaborate.

"I didn't have a girlfriend," Adam admitted. "I went out with many women, but there was no one special. Then there she was, sitting on the sand, all golden and brown. She was like honey to a bee and there was an entire hive of bees buzzing around her. I didn't think I had a chance. So I looked but didn't enter the fight for her attention."

"Before you knew it she was standing somewhere near you." Teddy completed the thought for him.

"Something like that," he said. "How did you know?"

"It's a woman thing." She left it at that.

"We didn't see each other after that. I met and married someone else. When that dissolved, I started my business. Getting it off the ground took all my time. One day Chloe came in with her aunt to talk about estate planning."

"You started seeing each other," Teddy stated.

Adam nodded. "I was working night and day, but she was there when I had free time. She was supportive, fun, easy to talk to. She even helped out just to be with me. I thought she was so different from Chelsea. She was interested in the business, interested in me."

"And so you fell in love," Teddy suggested.

"We did. And we were planning our wedding. We didn't have the white lace and orange blossoms. We were just going to go off one afternoon and get married."

"But that never happened?" Teddy questioned.

"We'd been dating a little over a year," Adam said.

He stopped and Teddy waited. Adam knew she thought there was more to the story. And there was.

"What happened?" she asked.

Even now, five years later he still found it hard to talk about. "Chloe was having an affair with another man. I found them together. We argued and she walked out on me."

Teddy gasped. "I am so sorry."

Adam didn't want to go on, but knew he had to. "When she left, we were both angry. She jumped in the car and took off. I thought she was alone but found out later she was with a guy. Less than a mile from our apartment, there was an accident. She'd driven too fast and lost control. It hit a telephone pole. Both of them died. The autopsy revealed she was pregnant. The child wasn't mine."

"Oh, my God," Teddy said. She reached for him, hugging him close and holding on, giving him the support he needed. "I can't imagine how you must have felt."

"It was hard for a time," he said. He kept his arms around her, took in the smell of her hair, the softness of her body. Teddy was nothing like Chloe. She was her own woman, with her own goals. She didn't attach herself to anyone like Chloe had done to him. Chloe had been content to hang on to his coattails, let him do the work and support her. She'd had little ambition and as soon as the ring was on her hand, she'd never come to the office again. Adam wondered if she'd ever loved him or if he just happened to be the one with the most potential.

He didn't look at Teddy. He knew he was in love with her, but she also scared him. Chloe had done a number on him and it wasn't Teddy's fault, but after his experience with his wife and then Chloe, could he trust another woman the way he'd trusted Chloe? When he'd taken his vows before God and their friends, he'd meant them. He fully expected to spend his life making Chelsea both rich and happy. That had changed. Then Chloe had come along and he felt as if this was real love. But that had collapsed, too. Veronica added to his vase of black roses. Like Chloe she'd betrayed him. But she didn't have her claws as deeply into him as his ex-fiancée had.

"I know what happened to you is hard to deal with," Teddy said. "And now I think I understand your mother better."

"My mother? How's that?"

"Chloe broke your trust. You were younger, less

experienced with the world. You grew up in that moment."

"I can't argue that," he said.

"You also decided to go it alone. Women weren't trustworthy. Even when you loved them, they would let you down."

Adam had never heard it put that way before. "That's not altogether true. I went out with plenty of women. I just never found the right one." He challenged Teddy's characterization.

"You didn't really want to. You used your job as a crutch to end a relationship. You used your past relationships as a reason to not risk your heart on another disappointment."

"I've been out with you more than any other woman," he said.

Teddy smiled. "Because I'm safe. We had an agreement from the beginning. There was no chance of us getting close to a relationship. No danger of me stepping across your line in the sand. No risk of me challenging your heart."

How wrong she was, Adam thought. She'd affected his heart more than any woman ever had. And that included Chloe. Adam couldn't say when it happened, but it had.

"You said something about my mother."

"Your mother's quest is to help you find someone to replace Chloe in your heart."

"I assure you, Chloe is no longer in my heart."

"Maybe," she said. "Maybe not."

"What about you?" Adam asked. "Is that guy still in your heart?"

"Chad? He was, but he's no longer part of my life. And he has no hold on me anymore."

He patted her hand. "We are a pair."

"But not a couple."

Chapter 10

Snow showed up for the holidays. It came down heavy, coating the ground and everything in its path. It was white and beautiful, but for Teddy it only added to her depression. By December 15, there were several layers on the ground and more coming.

She was in no mood for shopping, but staying home was worse. She opted for the shopping mall. She meandered through the stores, looking but not buying anything. Her mind wasn't on finding the perfect gift for loved ones. She'd had her gift. Had it and lost it. She looked at her naked hand. The engagement ring had been on her third finger only long enough for her to understand how much she'd miss it. While it had only been there a matter of hours, she now felt as if part of her hand had been removed.

Still, she had her love for Adam and there was nothing that could top that.

Nothing could change things, either. Picking up a purse, she opened it, thinking of her sister Sierra. Purses were Sierra's thing. A moment later Teddy shook her head and replaced it in the display. She had only ten days to finish her shopping, but she wasn't going to make any headway today.

Leaving the shopping mall, Teddy walked slowly to her car, unmindful of the falling snow. Her body was covered by the time she opened the door and slipped behind the wheel. As she pushed the ignition button, her phone rang. The radio panel lit up, indicating a call from Adam. Her heart jumped and she let out a small cry of delight when his name appeared on the screen.

What was wrong? she wondered. They had talked about things and parted. They were not a couple. Why was he calling? She pressed the screen, accepting the call.

"Yes," she said.

"Teddy?"

"Yes."

"Are you all right?"

Adam's voice caught her off guard, even though she knew he was calling. "I'm fine."

"Are you in your car?"

"Yes," she said.

"You're driving in this weather?"

She looked around the parking lot. Despite the snow, the lot was full. "Not yet. I just got in the car."

"Where are you?"

"At the mall. I went Christmas shopping." She didn't tell him she bought nothing. She didn't ask why he was calling. She only wanted to continue hearing his voice. "Where are you?"

"Home."

Teddy had nothing else to say. Time stretched between them.

"I'm calling about the invitation," Adam said.

"What invitation?"

"You've forgotten," he stated. "We were invited to Stephen and Erin's holiday party, the guy from my office. Is that still on?"

"You're right. I did forget."

"I know we're no longer pretending to be engaged, but we did accept the invitation. Do you think we should go or cancel?"

Her heart sang. She could spend another night with him. Maybe he'd look at her differently. She was no longer a means to an end. Maybe they could just go and enjoy themselves. Maybe they could begin again.

"Like a first date?" she teased, not knowing if her words would really sound that way through the wireless technology.

She heard him laugh. "We never did really have a first date, did we?"

"We'll go then?" she said.

"We'll go. I'll pick you up on Saturday at eight."

"I'll be ready," she said. They rang off. Teddy put the car in gear and drove to the offices of Weddings by Diana. She was suddenly grateful for all the December weddings. Grabbing her purse, she got out. Her feet practically flew through the snow.

She needed a new dress, and this was just where she could get it.

The suits Adam had chosen and discarded numbered six. Ralph Lauren, Hugo Boss, Gucci, Prada, Dolce & Gabbana, and Giorgio Armani lay on the bed, one or two having slipped to the floor. He held a Versace in his left hand and a Brioni in his right. Brioni won.

He wore excellent brands for client meetings, but tonight he wanted to look his best. It had been a while, a long while, since he dressed to impress. Yet he wanted to impress Teddy. Adam pulled the suit off the hanger and began dressing. He shrugged into a dress shirt and collected the cuff links Quinn had brought him back from Ireland three years ago.

Once he and Teddy's secret was out, things between them had fallen off track. He missed seeing her. They had been together for months, seen each other practically daily. He liked the way she laughed, how she seemed to pull life toward her and not complain about it. He liked that she embraced family. He liked that she coaxed him into remembering how happy a Christmas tree could make him. And their lovemaking was beyond describable. She was more than he expected and he wanted to keep seeing her. Maybe tonight they could compromise. Begin again. This time without the interference of parents. They could take it slowly. He was willing to go as slow as she wanted, *if* she wanted it at all.

The thought stopped him in his tracks.

He remembered their first night together. Neither wanted to go on a blind date, but even then he realized there was something about her that drew him. As time went by, seeing her more and more became the right thing to do. Then the revelation ripped them apart.

A pair, not a couple, she'd said. They were back to their normal lives. Only, for Adam, things were no longer normal. He wanted a new normal. He wanted to spend his days and nights with her. He wanted to go where life led them.

Tonight would be the first step.

By Saturday night Teddy had completely altered the designer gown. Standing in front of her bedroom mirror, she surveyed herself. The gown was chiffon. Christmas-green in color. The strapless bodice was completely made of green and white bugle beads. The skirt swished about her legs as if it wanted to dance. Her waist was defined by a wide red ribbon that formed a rose at the base of her back, its streamers falling to the floor in two sharp points.

She'd pulled her hair up on the sides and secured it with beaded combs that matched the gown. Curls cascaded down her back. Catching a wayward strand, she secured it and turned toward the door.

Adam was waiting for her downstairs. He looked up when he heard her footsteps. Words must have escaped him for his mouth dropped open and he stared at her as if he'd never seen her before.

"I'm sorry I kept you waiting," she said.

He came to her, taking her hand and looking her up and down. "It was well worth it."

Teddy heard a wealth of meaning in those few simple words. He leaned forward and touched her cheek with his.

"Clearly you'll be the best-looking woman at the party tonight."

"You think so?" she asked.

"I know so."

"Then undoubtedly we'll be the couple of the evening because you look good enough to eat."

The expression on his face darkened. She could see need flood his eyes. Teddy felt her own body begin to arouse.

"We'd better go," Adam said. "Although I would like nothing better than to skip the party and stay here."

Teddy wanted the same thing. "Would Stephen really mind if we didn't show up?"

Adam stared deeply into her eyes. "He'd consider it a snub. And I'm not sure what message it would send to the staff."

"Then we'd better go. We wouldn't want to start any rumors."

She reached for the coat she'd left lying over the sofa. Adam picked it up and held it for her. Teddy slipped her arms inside and Adam pulled it up onto her shoulders. His hands rested there for a moment. Teddy leaned back into him. Her eyes closed at the feel of his body. She remembered it, knew it, yearned for it. He encircled her upper arms and together they stood as one for a moment.

Teddy turned in his arms and lifted her head. She was about to tell Adam to let Stephen stew, when he stepped away.

The snow had stopped, but there was a layer still on the ground. The party was in full swing when they arrived. Adam introduced her to the hosts and they got a drink.

"These are the people you work with?" Teddy asked.

"A few are clients, but mainly it's the office personnel."

"So who's minding the store? I thought you ran a twenty-four-hour operation."

Taking a sip of his drink, he said, "There's a skeleton crew on duty. Things move slowly this time of year."

"Stephen has a beautiful home," she commented, looking around at the colonial. The decorations were beautiful and it appeared he had children. There were photographs on several of the tree ornaments.

"Shall we dance?" Adam interrupted her thoughts. She set her glass on a nearby tray and he took her into the room that had obviously been cleared for dancing. Couples were already on the floor and a DJ was handling the music.

In Adam's arms she floated away. Closing her eyes, she matched his steps. Just as she predicted, the dress danced. Teddy was only the medium who wore it, and she was the one feeling the security of being held by Adam. She took in the smell of his cologne, allowing the heady mixture to rekindle the sensations he brought out in her. Her mind wasn't thinking straight, but she had enough mental capacity left to let her know they were on a dance floor and not alone in her house or his condo.

When the music ended, she wished they could leave. She wanted to be alone with him, spend what little time they had left together, not in the midst of other people. Teddy noticed a woman looking at them. She smiled. The feeling that maybe the woman knew Adam suddenly made her jealous.

"Who is that?" she asked.

Adam looked in the direction Teddy indicated.

"She's a business associate. She works for the Princeton office of a large financial corporation. Why?"

"She's staring at us as if she knows a secret. Have you two dated?"

He smiled. "Jealous?"

The obvious hope in his voice wasn't lost on Teddy, however, she suspected it was laced with sarcasm. She reminded herself they were only here because of a previous agreement.

"You didn't answer my question."

"The answer is no. I never dated her."

Teddy looked back. The woman was gone. In her wake, she'd left a question in Teddy's mind. She put it aside and concentrated on Adam.

"Is this party an annual thing?"

Adam nodded. "Stephen and his wife have hosted it each year since he came to work for me. Even before then."

"Have you come each year?"

"Most of them. There were times when I was out of the country, but if I was in town, I was here."

A steady stream of people came over to talk to Adam. He introduced her each time. He was the owner so it was natural that people would seek his attention. Teddy was getting a bad feeling as the night wore on. She thought they were more interested in her than in talking to Adam. Yet she didn't feel that it was the kind of curiosity about who the boss was seeing. There was an undertone she couldn't define.

After several conversations, Adam asked her to dance again. She went easily into his arms. That was where she wanted to be. They danced the same as before, only this time Teddy kept her eyes open and checked the other dancers. She noticed several people turning to stare at them and then whispering. She wondered what was wrong.

Excusing herself, she went to the ladies' room to check her makeup. Before she turned the corner she'd been directed to, she heard two women talking. And then she knew the reason for all the stares.

"Did you see her?" someone whispered.

"I did. She's stunning. I can see why Adam has her on his arm," another woman spoke.

"I wish he'd put me on his arm," the first one replied.

"If you have to compare yourself with her, you'd lose every time. This flavor has all the others beat by a mile."

All the others, Teddy was appalled. Arm candy! They thought she was arm candy.

Teddy wanted to say something, confront the two women. She wanted to let them know that she had a brain and that she and Adam were not an item. But what could she say? She didn't really know Adam. They had exchanged things about each other, about their pasts, but they hadn't talked about common interests. She knew women fawned all over him, obviously staring at him even when she walked with him. She didn't know his past. Other than Chelsea, Chloe and Veronica—and Veronica was definitely eye candy— Teddy didn't know that he'd dated enough women that his employees considered them nothing but the current fruit of the season. This included her. And she didn't like it. She didn't want to be lumped together with an invisible class of women who were interested in nothing more than being seen with a good-looking man.

When she reentered the party, she ran into Stephen.

"Having a good time?" he asked.

"Wonderful," she lied, but her smile was in place. Calling on her customer service background, she didn't want to let him know how she really felt.

"Let me get you a drink."

They weren't far from a bar that had been set up for the night. "White wine," she said, and Stephen raised his finger indicating he'd like one, too.

"Adam says you have this party every year," she opened with the first thing that came to mind.

"We do. My wife says it reminds her of the parties she went to during this time when she was younger."

"We used to go to a lot of parties during this season, too," Teddy told him.

"Now we work all the time," Stephen said.

"Adam said his hours are erratic."

The bartender set their glasses on the bar and they took them, moving away so another couple could order drinks.

"His are. For the rest of us, he tries as much as possible to keep us on domestic accounts so we can go home at reasonable hours."

"Doesn't leave much time for a social life," she said under her breath, then realized he heard her.

"He does all right," Stephen said.

Teddy decided to change the subject. She didn't want any of her feelings coming through after what she'd heard earlier.

"You like working for Adam?"

He nodded. "It's the best job I ever had. And even though I have some late nights, it's worth it."

Teddy looked past Stephen to where Adam stood. He was in the middle of a crowd where a lively discussion was going on. She noticed the two women she'd heard earlier were part of the group around him. She wondered which one wanted to be the arm candy.

"You're a wedding consultant," Stephen stated.

She nodded, taking a sip of her wine.

"From what I can tell, you're doing very well."

"What does that mean?" she asked.

"We've done some research into the financials. You seem to be on solid ground."

"Did Adam order that?"

"Not directly. We keep track of many small businesses. 'Small' means under twenty million in assets.

Weddings by Diana crossed my desk. But since you aren't a client, we're limited to only public information."

Teddy threw another glance at Adam. The crowd had moved away and he was coming toward her. Stephen's wife reached them at the same time.

"Adam, congratulations. I just heard you two are engaged." She looked from him to Teddy and back. "I must admit, I didn't think anyone would get you."

Teddy looked at the floor, then back up.

"We're not engaged," Adam said.

"You're not, but I…"

"We're not," Teddy confirmed.

"I'm sure there's a stadium of women who'll be glad to hear that," Stephen said.

Teddy felt the color drain from her face. Stephen's wife poked him in the side.

"I apologize," he said. "I didn't mean that the way it sounded."

"It's a long story." Adam protected her from further comments about their engagement. She was obviously embarrassed. "One night after I've had too many drinks, I might tell it to you." He glanced at Teddy. "But right now, I'm going to dance with the most beautiful woman at the party." He smiled at Teddy. She returned it even though there was no humor behind the gesture.

Adam took her arm and they headed for the dance floor, leaving a surprised host and hostess behind them. As soon as he turned her into his embrace, he said, "You and Stephen were deep in conversation."

Teddy missed a step and her shoe ended up on his.

"Sorry," she said and resumed. She placed her head next to his so he couldn't see her face.

"What were you talking about?"

"Working conditions, financial research and you." She tightened her arms.

Adam probably felt the change in her. She was stiff and she clutched him too close.

"Are you all right?" he asked. His voice was right at her ear.

She shook her head as much as she could move it. "I want to go," Teddy said.

"Why? What happened?"

"Please, let's leave."

"Don't let what Stephen said upset you."

"It's not Stephen," she said.

Adam sighed. "I'll say our good-nights and get your coat."

The woman Adam helped into the car was a direct opposite of the one who'd gotten in three hours ago. Silently they drove back to her house. Teddy didn't wait for him to come around and help her out. She stepped into the snow, unmindful of her shoes or the care she'd taken for their first date.

"Are you going to tell me what happened?"

Teddy reached her door and opened it. Inside Adam closed it and waited for her to speak.

"Why don't we just forget everything. The engagement is over. The party is over. We've completed our commitments. Let's just say goodbye and forget this ever happened."

"No." His voice held a finality to it. He was not

going to be easily pushed aside. "You talked to Stephen and everything changed. What did he say?"

"Stephen said nothing out of the ordinary. He told me about his job, about researching Weddings by Diana."

"And that upset you?"

"It's not about Stephen!" she shouted.

"Then what? His wife was misinformed about the engagement and the comment about a stadium of women…"

"It was none of that." Teddy looked at Adam. "Good night," she said.

Adam stared at her as if he could force her to explain. Teddy opened the door and he walked out.

"Goodbye," she whispered after he'd gone.

The "Wedding March" began. The doors opened and the bride and her father stood there. The sound of approval flew up from the crowded church as the congregation stood and the bride began her procession down the aisle.

Teddy felt tears mist her eyes. She blinked them away. This was the second wedding this month and it was the second time since she and Diana began their business that Teddy found herself moved by the ceremony.

She was aware of every word spoken, every sound of the organ, every gasp of the audience. And for the first time Adam's comments came back to her while she watched the bride. *Not once have you ever imagined it would one day be your turn?*

She imagined it now. She wanted to be the bride, wanted to float down that aisle with her one and only waiting for her.

Adam was her one and only.

But for him, Chloe was The One. She was the reason Adam swore off relationships. He didn't even realize it, but Chloe had changed him. She'd taken away his ability to trust anyone except himself. And he didn't realize it. To him, Teddy was only arm candy.

Teddy had felt the same when Chad betrayed her. She hadn't sworn off relationships, but she was much more particular than she had been before. Then Adam walked into her life. Reluctantly at first, but he'd taken up a large amount of space in her heart and he was unaware of it.

How much easier it would be if Veronica had been her competition. Teddy wished she was. Veronica was alive. Chloe was a ghost. Trying to exorcise a ghost was nearly impossible. Chloe had a hold on Adam's mind, and she was unchanging. He probably went through scenarios regularly of what he could have done differently. Why did she take a lover? Why wasn't he enough for her? That was the hardest question. And it had no answer. He couldn't remove the outcome of their argument. She'd gotten into that car and driven too fast. And she would never be there to explain, to relieve him of the guilt he felt over her death.

It was up to Teddy to fill that role. And she was going to do it.

"Teddy?" Renee's voice came through her earpiece. "Are you there?"

Teddy didn't know how many times her consultant had called her name. She was lost in her own thoughts.

"I'm here."

"Is the photographer in place?"

Teddy looked down the long aisle. "He's near the front."

"Good. The bride wanted to make sure there were photos of the actual ceremony."

Teddy knew the photographer. She'd worked with him many times and recommended him whenever asked. "She has nothing to worry about."

"Is everything all right with you?"

"I was a little distracted, but everything is in order."

Teddy had been thinking of Adam. The church wasn't Saint Patrick's Cathedral, yet Teddy continually looked around for Adam. He'd surprised her by showing up for one of her weddings. She wondered, hoped, he would do it again. But the ceremony was practically over and he had not shown.

Skipping the reception, Teddy opted to pack up and drive home. She hoped Adam would be waiting for her. But her driveway was empty when she reached it. They no longer had a reason to meet each other. Their parents knew the engagement was a sham. Adam had a business to run. As did she. Their agreement had come to an end. It was time to move on.

Teddy had been at this crossroad many times. Never had it been a problem to throw herself into her designs. Her concentration might be off for a day, but she would forget and go on. She had a sinking feeling this was not the case today.

Entering the house, she felt an echo of emptiness. She and Adam hadn't been there together that often, but they'd had breakfast in her kitchen, made love in her bedroom, kissed in her living room. Suddenly, she didn't want to be there alone. She could call Diana. Scott was out of town. The two could go for a drink. Teddy shook her head, discarding the idea. She was in no mood to be with other people. Diana would immediately sense her mood and ply her with questions on her feelings for Adam.

Those feelings were in chaos.

She wondered where he was. Was he at his office? It wasn't that late, only a little past seven in the evening. The international markets were open. He could be working. Teddy didn't call any of the phone numbers she had for him. She decided to take a bath and go to bed early, but once she stepped out of the tub, she knew she wouldn't be able to sleep.

Adam was on her mind. Was he all right? Could he be feeling the way she was? The two of them had agreed to a plan and now that was over. So why did Teddy feel as if she'd lost a friend?

Chapter 11

"The Nokamara stock opened three dollars higher than yesterday's closing."

Adam looked up. Stephen Bryant stood in front of him. He hadn't heard anything the man had said. In fact, he didn't know how long he'd been standing there.

"You look sick," Stephen said. "Maybe you should go home. We can handle things here."

Adam sat at his desk. His mind wasn't on business and he wasn't ill. He was aware that his vice president could handle things. In the past few months while Adam spent all his time with Teddy, Stephen had held things down. But Adam was back now. Teddy was in the past. Their agreement was over. Yet he was having a hard time getting back into the swing of office routine.

"I'll be all right," Adam said. "Now, what did you say?"

"Nothing important," Stephen said. "I apologize for what I said at the party."

Stephen had apologized hundreds of time since the party, even though Adam told him he had not offended Teddy. Something had, but still he didn't know what it was.

"Think about going home," Stephen said.

He left and Adam did think about going home, but it no longer felt as if it belonged to him. Teddy's ghost lingered in the rooms. He could almost smell her unique fragrance when he sat on the sofa, hear the smile in her voice when she talked.

"I think you should call her."

This time Adam did hear the voice. He looked up to find Quinn standing in the doorway.

"What are you doing here?" he asked. "Don't you have a job to do?" Adam got up and rounded the desk to bear-hug his brother.

"If you'd look at the calendar, you'd know it's the week before Christmas. Many people take vacation at this time of year."

"And many take it after Christmas."

"But you work 365 days a year. At least you had before Teddy. But now…" He let the sentence linger.

"She and I are done. We were only together to thwart Mom. And we know how that ended."

Quinn whistled. "I'm amazed you're still able to walk around on this earth. Is Mom speaking to you yet?"

"Barely. We've had a few conversations. They were short and stilted."

"I'm sure she'll forgive you soon." He paused. "Especially if you call Teddy and get things back to the way they should be."

"Why would I do that?"

"Because you're miserable without Teddy. You can't concentrate. I bet you haven't really eaten in a while, you look haggard and you said you were in love with her."

"I never said that," Adam protested.

"Not in words, but it's obvious in everything you do and say."

Adam didn't want to hear the answer to the question that was on his mind. But Quinn went on.

"You've begun to lose weight."

Adam looked at himself and then at his brother.

"Only a pound or two, but the spiral has begun. You don't sleep. You look like a dead man walking. So why don't you do yourself a favor and go tell the woman you love her."

"I can't."

"Why not? It's only three little words."

"And it's not like I haven't said them before," Adam said.

Quinn frowned. "There's no reason to think Teddy will be anything like Veronica or Chloe."

"No indication, but there is one problem."

"What's that?" Quinn asked.

"She's not in love with me. She wouldn't even tell me what happened the night of Stephen's party. She said good-night, got out of the car, and I haven't talked to her since."

"You're sure about this? Because from what I saw of the two of you, there was no one else in the room when you were there. I could say the entire planet was inhabited by only the two of you."

Adam knew that was how he felt. When he was with her there was no other world except the one that enclosed them.

"You already bought the ring," Quinn reminded him. "Mom saw it. Even though she was angry, beyond angry—her words—she didn't miss a detail."

"I could talk to her if she isn't at a wedding. She had four of them this month," Adam said.

"And Christmas is coming. And the clocks will stop. And the world will end. Don't put obstacles in your way. It's not like you."

Adam questioned what he was like. Since meeting Teddy, much about him had changed. He supposed falling in love did that to a person. Could Quinn be right? Had Teddy fallen in love with him?

There was only one way to find out.

Adam practiced his speech in front of his bathroom mirror. He repeated it while he dressed in a suit and tie. In the living room, he went over it again while looking for the keys to his car. During the drive to her office, he had committed it to memory and was sure of what he wanted to say. Pulling into the parking lot, panic set in. He hadn't accounted for her replies. He should have a plan for what her responses could be.

But he was too late. Teddy appeared at the door and walked toward him. She smiled broadly and as Quinn had predicted, the world around them disappeared. He couldn't see her curves because of the coat she wore, but Adam knew them intimately, and as she walked into his arms, he encircled her waist and she kissed him on the cheek. He held her a moment longer than necessary, inhaling her perfume and wanting to press her to him until the world tilted back in place.

"Don't you look like a member of the wedding." She stepped back and looked him over.

He knew she was talking about the suit, but the comment affected him as if she'd gone straight for the heart.

"I was surprised to hear from you." He opened the car door and she got in. "But I needed to get out of the office for a while."

"The weddings?" he asked.

"It seems all the brides want to change something at the last minute." She glanced at him as he pulled the car out of the parking lot. "But I don't want to talk about weddings. How have you been?"

"I miss our *dates*," he said honestly. Adam couldn't look at her long enough to gauge the expression on her face.

"They were fun." She laughed. Sobering, she asked, "How are things with your mom?"

"We're talking."

He pulled into the parking lot of his condo.

"We're having lunch here?" Teddy asked in surprise.

"I want to talk to you and I don't want a lot of people around."

Silently they walked up the few steps to the condo's entry. Inside, he took her coat and led her to the dining room.

"Wow!" Teddy said.

The table was set for two with candles lit and the food hot and ready. A flower arrangement made of pine branches, Christmas holly and mistletoe sat in the center, replacing the silver bells that she'd set there. The napkins were folded into shapes that looked like white doves. Christmas music played softly in the background. Everything was as he'd ordered it.

"How did you do this?" She smiled, obviously pleased. She touched the silverware and bent to smell the pine in the centerpiece.

Adam smiled, too. Involuntarily, a lightning bolt went through him. Forcing himself to stand his ground, he remembered his speech, but it wasn't time yet. He wasn't comfortable. This was unchartered ground and he found it hard to relax. "I had it catered. Quinn was here to supervise. He ducked out the moment we pulled in the lot."

Teddy nodded her approval.

"This looks like a very special occasion."

"Sit down."

He helped her into the chair and took his seat next to her. She opened the cover on her plate. "Duck à l'orange," he supplied.

"This conversation must really be something important," she said, taking a bite of the food. Her eyes swept down, revealing her appreciation of the succulent meat. Adam loved the way she did that. He'd seen her in the throes of passion and this compared with that expression. The thought aroused him.

Tamp it down, he told himself.

"You like the food?" Adam said.

"I love duck à l'orange." Teddy took another bite. "And this is excellent. Who catered this?"

One hurdle reached, he thought. This was the opening. It was what he was waiting for, but every word he'd practiced disappeared as if it was in a foreign language. One he didn't speak.

"Adam," Teddy called him.

"I'm getting married," he blurted out.

She didn't choke, but she came close. "What!"

"I'm thinking of having this as an entrée at the reception."

"Reception?" Teddy dropped her fork. It clattered against the china before settling on the white tablecloth.

"I'm getting married again. I'd like to hire Weddings by Diana to plan the wedding."

She sat back in the chair. "I should have brought a pad for notes," she said flatly. "I suppose congratulations are in order." She stood up, taking her wineglass with her as she moved away from the table. She hadn't touched it since they sat down, but must have needed it now. Raising it, she toasted him. The drink she took was long. She drained the glass and set it down next to her uneaten food. Turning away from the table, she moved to the archway between the kitchen and dining room. "Shouldn't I talk to the bride about the services we provide?"

"I'm sure you know them well enough to choose."

"I don't understand."

Adam moved from his seat at one end of the table to come and stand in front of Teddy. Taking her hands, he pulled her close.

"I love you," he said. "Quinn says you're in love with me, too. Is it true?"

Her eyes widened. They were clear and he held them, waiting for her to say something.

"I thought you weren't looking for a wife, just someone to please your mother."

"That was true in the beginning."

"And now?"

The words were delivered slowly, but the weight they carried was immeasurable. "Now I know she chose the right woman for me," Adam said.

"Are you sure?" Teddy asked. "This isn't another one of your schemes to get back into good graces with your mother, is it?"

Instead of answering, Adam put his hands on both sides of her head and pulled her mouth to his. He felt her surrender almost immediately. Her arms went around his waist and he deepened the kiss. His tongue swept into her mouth, drinking in the taste of her.

He felt as if years had passed since the last time he had her in his arms, since he could take in the smell of her shampoo, since he could revel in the nectar that was uniquely hers. Frenzy overtook him and he devoured her mouth. He wanted to get closer to her, wanted to speak to her through his kisses, through the texture of her hair, the smoothness of her skin. He wanted all of her.

Raising his head, he mumbled against her mouth, "I love you. I think I have since the first night we met." His voice was breathy, forcing him to speak in staccato measures. He looked deeply into her eyes. "You were leaving the restaurant and I didn't want you to go. I couldn't let you walk away so quickly. Despite the setup by our mothers, I felt the spark."

He kissed her again. Quinn had to be right. There was no way she could kiss him like this and not feel something for him. No way she could look at him the way she did and not feel the same way he did.

This time she pushed him back. Dropping her head, she took a long breath, then looked directly in his eyes. "I love you, too," she said.

Adam thought his legs would give out. He'd longed to hear her say it, but he was unsure until this very moment.

"I thought you were against marriage," Teddy said. "You told me that the first night we met. Then there's Veronica and Chloe, women who broke your heart and made you mistrustful of women."

"I know." He remembered their conversations, yet his voice held a bit of humor. "They tainted my views for a while, but there comes a time when you have to take a chance. Risk whatever is necessary for the promise of happiness."

"You're willing to do that for me?"

"That and more," he said, dropping a kiss on her nose.

"I don't think there will be much risk," Teddy assured him. "I love you and nothing will change that."

"There's only one thing missing," Adam said.

"What?"

He released her for a moment and went to the table in the living room. Retrieving a small box from the drawer, he brought it back to her. Adam lifted the black velvet cover. The Varrick name was emblazoned on the inside lid.

"My ring," she said.

He removed it. "You will marry me." He stated it as a foregone conclusion.

"I will," Teddy said.

He slipped the heavy stone on her finger. This time it meant more to both of them than it had in the past. When they chose it, Teddy had protested. But this time their engagement was real and the ring was real.

They sealed the engagement with a kiss.

The bed wasn't just in disarray. It had been destroyed. The sheets were hanging off the sides or completely removed from the mattress.

Adam caught one of the linens and covered them with it. Teddy's heart was beating double time, her body was bathed in a sheen of sweat, but she was happier than she'd ever been.

Adam lay beside her, cradling her in his arms, one hand on her breast. She'd asked herself if their lovemaking would equal the first time. Then the second. Would it always be this intense, this thoroughly satisfying? She couldn't answer that, but she hoped it would.

"You know no one is going to believe us when we

tell them we're engaged," she told him. Her voice was deep with sexual satisfaction.

He nodded against her hair. "They'll think it's another trick."

Teddy stretched her hand out admiring the ring. "We can't even show them a different ring." She laughed. "Maybe they'll believe us on our tenth anniversary."

"Do you want a different ring?"

He pushed back and looked over her shoulder. "Absolutely not."

"Whether they believe it or not, we'll know," Adam said and pulled her back closer to his naked body. Teddy felt the rise in heat, the familiar burn that accompanied arousal.

She turned over. He brushed her hair from her face and gazed at her. She could see the need in his eyes, feel the desire in the strength of his body.

"Your hair is a complete mess," he whispered as he threaded his fingers through it. Over and over, he combed the strands as if they were gold. His mouth kissed her face, skipping from place to place.

"I have you to thank for my messy hair," Teddy said. "Thank you." Her murmur was low and sexy, conveying everything she felt, everything that he brought out in her.

Adam took a moment to stare at her. Tension built within her as he watched, held her with only his eyes for a thousand years. Teddy's mouth went dry. She licked her lips to wet them. He lowered his mouth, replacing her tongue. Their lips mated and clung. Arms and legs circled and entwined, bringing their bodies into alignment. Teddy ran her legs up and down against him, touching in the most intimate way. Fire sprang up like meteors hitting the ground. She ached for him, to have him close, inside her, to feel the presence of his body joined with hers. She wanted the unbottled elixir they created. It was around them, holding them together. It was not for sale and had a shelf life of less than an hour, but it generated feelings so strong and so passionate that Teddy could die from continued exposure. Yet she wanted the elixir, wanted to open it, relive its effect at any moment of the day or night.

She felt the joy of penetration when they joined, the beginning of a dance that would take her to places never before found by anyone except the two of them.

His body drove into hers and she met him with each deep and soulful thrust. Her hips lifted off the bed, slamming into him, taking him inside to the hilt of his sex, draining whatever pleasure he offered. She took and she gave. Together they determined their own rhythm. It started on an upbeat and went up from there, going from frenzied to wicked as they mounted the levels of hedonism.

The room filled with the electric snap of lovers mating. Waves of emotion thundered inside her, crashing and reforming with the velocity of tidal waves. The seas of a primitive dance swirled and burst into raining fountains. Hands raked her sides and gathered her behind as Adam guided her up and into the heights of mutual love.

Teddy gasped for air but refused to stop the raging storm rocketing through her body. And then a new feeling took over. She was aware of everything about herself, not only the overwhelming pleasure that she and Adam forged, but every blood vessel, every nerve, the feel of Adam's hands on her, the softness of the mattress beneath her, and the deluge of powerful emotions that assaulted her senses and crossed her over into a land of pure sensation. Her scream came loud and long as she reached the height of ecstasy.

Together they fell back to earth, coming down fast and hard. Breath shallow and panting, her heart throbbing, Teddy tried to calm herself. Adam's weight pressed her into the bed, kept her warm. She wanted his weight, triumphed in the compassionate nature of this one and only. His arms enclosed her, holding on to a nebulous thread that bonded them together. For a moment longer, she wanted to resist the slowing of the sensation that connected them.

Adam rolled off her, pulling her into his side. He faced her, his eyes drowsy and his mouth curved in a half smile.

"I love you," he said.

Epilogue

The gown Teddy designed for her own wedding was her best effort ever. She used Viennese lace and bolts of satin. The dress fitted to her waist, the skirt was straight in the front, but the back bustled out into a train that rivaled anything she'd seen anywhere. Pearls and crystals covered the entire dress and glittered in the candlelit church. Her veil draped down her back and extended several feet beyond the train.

The two mothers proved the rule by challenging everything. The bridesmaids' veils didn't match the dresses. Should they wear hats and not veils? It was a June wedding so the men should be dressed in a lighter color, not the traditional black with white tie and tails. They went on and on, and Teddy felt sorry for Lisa, the wedding consultant handling the arrangements. Often she or Adam were called on to provide the deciding vote or to placate the mothers. But when it came to the ceremony, they were there with smiles on.

Lisa had the privilege of dealing with the mother of the bride and the mother of the groom—a fate that certainly proved her worth.

The organ music began. Teddy heard it from the vestibule where she stood. Diana looked at her and smiled. Renee and Teddy's two sisters were her bridesmaids. They gave her a final nod and started down the aisle. Diana, as matron of honor, followed them.

"Well, honey, I promise not to cry, but you look wonderful," her mother said and hugged her. Normally, the mother of the bride began the ceremony by being escorted to her seat by a groomsman. Teddy's father had that honor. Teddy would walk down the aisle escorted by her mother. Teddy had asked her mother to divert from tradition and give her away. Gemma Granville happily cried at the honor.

The "Wedding March" began. Both women looked at each other. Mist was in her mother's eyes. Teddy had heard that music a hundred times at other weddings. Today it sounded for her. Her heartbeat quickened. On the other side of that door stood Adam waiting for her. She loved him more than she ever thought possible. Moments from now they would be husband and wife.

The church was full, adorned with fragrant flowers and lighted with candles. There was a rolled out white carpet strewn with long-stemmed red roses that led to the altar.

Gemma Granville's arm trembled as the two stepped on the carpet and began their walk.

Teddy and Adam pledged their troth and the groom kissed the bride.

* * * * *

She had only herself to rely on...until a wounded soldier offered his friendship...and ecstasy beyond her dreams.

JERICHO

GINGER JAMISON

Georgia Williams has traveled a hard road from sheltered preacher's daughter to struggling single mother. As a night nurse at Jericho Military Hospital, she meets Lieutenant Christian Howard—a man of duty, honor and deep desires. Something about the scarred war hero touches Georgia, awakening feelings she's tried to keep hidden. But one passionate night changes everything, erupting with consequences neither could have foreseen.

"Complex, engrossing novel." —*RT Book Reviews* on *Liberty*

Available September 2014 wherever books are sold!

Can he convince her to take another chance on love?

ESSENCE **BESTSELLING AUTHOR**

GWYNNE FORSTER

McNEIL'S *MATCH*

After a bitter divorce, twenty-nine-year-old Lynne Thurston is faced with the prospect of not knowing what to do with the rest of her life. Once a highly ranked pro tennis player, she gave it all up six years ago when she got married. Now with nothing else to lose, can she make a comeback on the tennis circuit? Sloan McNeil is a businessman who wants to convince Lynne that she still has what it takes... both on *and* off the court!

> "Caring and sensitive...FLYING HIGH is a moving story fit for any keeper shelf."
> —*RT Book Reviews*

Available September 2014 wherever books are sold!

Is it a summer fling...or the beginning of forever?

ESSENCE BESTSELLING AUTHOR

DONNA HILL

FOR YOU I *Will*

After ten years of service as an E.R. chief at a New York City hospital, Dr. Kai Randall decided to trade her scrubs for a calmer existence in Sag Harbor Village. Still, a photo she snapped of a handsome, solitary stranger continues to haunt her. But that's nothing compared to how she feels when she comes face-to-face with the man from her dreams, Assistant District Attorney Anthony Weston. Although Anthony's life is in turmoil, could the soul-stirring passion they share be the beginning of a new life together?

"Yum! This novel in the Sag Harbor Village series is smooth and sexy like dark chocolate!"
—*Book Reviews* on *Touch Me Now*

Available September 2014 wherever books are sold!

REQUEST YOUR FREE BOOKS!

2 FREE NOVELS
PLUS 2 FREE GIFTS!

KIMANI™
ROMANCE

Love's ultimate destination!

If she's going to win, she needs to play the game…

Seduced
BY THE PLAYBOY

Pamela Yaye

Newscaster Angela Kelly wants to take the Windy City by storm. But with her show's low ratings, she stands to lose everything. An exposé on professional baseball player Demetri Morretti might be her last shot. But when Angela finds herself in danger, Demetri will have to prove there's more to him than just his playboy status….

"A page-turner from start to finish…a great story."
—*RT Book Reviews* on *GAMES OF THE HEART*

The Morretti Millionaires

HARLEQUIN®
www.Harlequin.com

Available now!

They still burn for
each other....

Indulge ME TONIGHT

ALTONYA WASHINGTON

Graedon Clegg has misgivings about a weeklong retreat with his estranged brother. One, his brother can't be trusted. And two, it's hosted by Grae's ex-wife, Tielle…and he still burns for her. Tielle is delighted to help heal their family, and having powerful, handsome Grae around again is painful yet exciting and tempting. Now, in the same place they honeymooned, will their new time together rekindle the romance they once shared?

"This story moves at a great pace, and the sights and sounds leap off
the pages, allowing readers to feel connected to the story."
—*RT Book Reviews* on *Trust In Us*

www.Harlequin.com

Available September 2014
wherever books are sold!

KPAW3720914

They are political rivals...until the doors are closed!

SECRET SILVER *Nights*

ZURI DAY

Nico Drake dreams of one day becoming governor of his state. First item on his agenda? Beating his newest mayoral challenger, Monique Slater. She has big plans for their small town, and they don't include falling for her sexy political rival. Keeping their sizzling relationship under wraps while running against each other is a tightrope act, but can Monique convince Nico that there are no losers when it comes to love?

The Drakes of California

"Day's love scenes are fueled by passion and the tale will keep readers on their toes until the very end."
—*RT Book Reviews* on *Diamond Dreams*

HARLEQUIN®
™ www.Harlequin.com

Available September 2014 wherever books are sold!

KPZD3700914